these

TIES

WE

FORGE

PRAISE FOR

THESE TIES WE FORGE

"*These Ties We Forge* offers a close-up look to children in need and how we can meet those needs. With stories and poems that dive into topics on rejection, love, loss, and healing, *These Ties We Forge* is a compelling tribute and stirring collection."

—Caitlin Miller, Author of *The Memories We Painted* and *Our Yellow Tape Letters*

"A heartfelt collection of poems and short stories that explores the family we forge, find, and fight for—and the sacrifices required to keep it safe. This anthology beautifully celebrates the life-giving love of family in many forms."

—Beka Gremikova, Author of *Unexpected Encounters of a Draconic Kind and Other Stories*

"Wonderfully crafted and inspiring, *These Ties We Forge* is a heartfelt anthology of stories surrounding the difficult circumstances faced by children around the world. It encapsulates the hope we find in Christ and the difference one person can make in the lives of the lost."

—Xanna Renae, Author of *Down with the Prince*

these

TIES

WE

FORGE

Anne J. Hill ● Natalie Noel Truitt

Morgan J. Manns ● Nathaniel Luscombe

Yvonne McArthur ● Hannah Carter ● H. L. Davis

Sarah Anne Elliott ● Andrea Renae ● D. T. Powell

Denica McCall ● Annie Louise Twitchell ● Jade La Grange

Brooke J. Katz ● AudraKate Gonzalez ● C. F. Barrows

Shana Burchard ● Maseeha Seedat ● Ali Noël

These Ties We Forge

Copyright ©2024 Anne J. Hill

Printed in the United States of America

Paperback ISBN: 978-1-956499-21-6

Originally published in April 2024
Published by Twenty Hills Publishing

Cover Art by JV Arts
Interior formatting by Andrea Renae

Edited by Anne J. Hill, Natalie Noel Truitt,
Samantha Mendell, and Claire Tucker

Book created by Anne J. Hill, head of Twenty Hills Publishing,
with the help of Natalie Noel Truitt

Anne J. Hill:
To my family and friends in South Africa

Natalie Noel Truitt:
To Ollie and Thea. May you have thousands of bright days

TABLE OF CONTENTS

"Defend the poor and fatherless:
do justice to the afflicted and needy.
Deliver the poor and needy:
rid them out of the hand of the wicked."

Psalm 82:3-4 (KJV)

INTRODUCTION

Thank you so much for picking up a copy of this book. It means the world to me and your financial support is a blessing. I've had a heart for orphans and helping children in general ever since going to South Africa and volunteering at a baby home (a home that cares for babies who, for various reasons, cannot be cared for by their parents.) My brother and his family are working to move to South Africa (his wife's homeland) and work with this same ministry.

A good portion of royalties from two of our other books, *Tales of Many* books one and two, already support these two baby homes directly, one book per home. A percent of the royalties for this book will go toward supporting my brother and his family as they do mission work in South Africa—one of their main areas of focus will be living at and overseeing one of the baby homes. Whenever they finish their work there, the royalties will then go toward the ministry as a whole, other missionaries that are connected to the ministry, the baby homes, or specific needs. No matter what, the funds will go toward One Hope For Africa (also known as 1Hope Ministries.)

I wanted to create a book that portrays some of the needs children going through difficult times have and bring hope to anyone who has been in that position or knows someone who has. The stories vary between genres, some fantastical and some realistic, but all of them show children in need and someone attempting to meet those needs. My hope is that it will also stir others to help where they can and go deeper in caring for children.

—Anne J. Hill

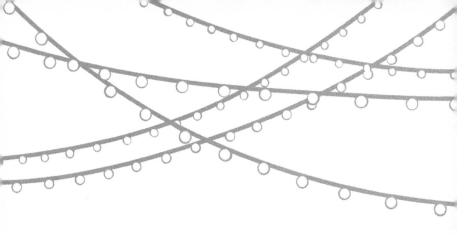

OTO-SAN

ANDREA RENAE

Each hour passes like a shock through the man's core. His knees bounce, shaking the bench. Disgruntled glares fire at him, but he fixes his sight on the garish green numbers and waits for his stop.

It will be ages.

The cabin is like a mausoleum, unnaturally deadened. He battles the urge to hum or cough or sigh—anything to drown out the clamor of time unwinding. Of his past rushing to meet him.

Tick. Tick.

An acrid scent wafts, churning the man's empty stomach. The old vessel, crammed with strangers, is suffocating. People sway in unison as the ship shudders through pockets of temporal turbulence. Every few minutes, someone reaches up and tugs their cord, stopping the motion and the flickering clock. Fresh air rushes in as the door screeches open, the man gulping it in as he observes the other passengers' expressions. Some look hopeful, even excited. Others are hard, determined. Many faces shine with tears.

He resolves to feel nothing. *At least not yet.*

As the timecraft powers up again with a weary lurch, he pulls out a worn paper barely holding together at the creases. His fingers trace the faded image of a woman on a stretcher, her beauty marred by the touch of death. She is supposed to be nameless, a nobody. A grim face to enhance a shocking headline spun to sell the news. But she is not no one to him, and he cannot bear to look at her. The man's eyes anchor on the words instead, and he inhales sharply, as if he hasn't read them a hundred times.

ICHIOYASHIDE VIOLENCE ON THE RISE: CHANCELLOR TO HOLD FORUM TO REVERSE BANE ON THE UNWANTED.

Too late . . . too late, he thinks.

A child across the aisle whimpers, breaking him from his daze. He blinks a few times, watching the girl slump and drop a cracked tablet into a bag at her feet. Her bottom lip protrudes; she seems to be ten *ticks* away from a complete meltdown.

The man's toes curl inside his polished shoes. *Why would*

anyone drag someone so young through this ordeal? Surely, a child cannot be expected to abide by the laws of time. One simple action can have a ripple effect that will wipe her from existence.

He assesses the haggard woman next to her, whose face twists as she watches the clock reverse. One hand constricts around a purse handle, and the other rests protectively over the back of the girl's seat.

At least the child has someone who cares for her.

Condemnation presses on the man's chest so that he cannot breathe until the girl's eyes seek his face. Throat loosening, he offers her a shy wink. She stares for several *ticks*, then abandons her slouch and tips forward, shoving her hands between her legs and the sticky seat.

"When will you get off?" Her timid voice dredges up the emotions the old man has been so desperate to pack away.

The mosaic of people blurs before him, knit together by their shared desperation. It doesn't matter what circumstances drove them here because they are all the same.

The voyage on the timecraft could cost everything.

Tick. Tick.

The man avoids the girl's probing eyes and smears his tears away, tucking the paper back in his pocket. His words escape as a pained whisper.

"On the day I met my daughter."

Raindrops embedded themselves in Akari's threadbare silk dress like stings of hornets as she hurried from the market. She could hardly see the street, but that wasn't the rain's fault. A foul odor from an open doorway found her, followed by a suggestive whistle. She sped up a few paces to get out of the building's shadow as her stomach lurched.

It had taken her ten years to find him. The man called Saito Haru. Akari didn't know what she had expected. Maybe an apology for abandoning a young pregnant woman almost two decades ago. Maybe some hint of remorse for condemning a child to the *ichioyashide,* the magical bane that branded and restricted the unwanted. Even if society accepted her, Akari would be prevented from earning a single coin with the bane in place now that she was of age. The *ichioyashide* was a death sentence for an adult, and yet the man did not care. Neither did he seem bothered to learn that her mother had died after he left her. Callously dismissing her suffering, he had mocked Akari's insistence that he should claim her as his daughter.

Her only hope for lifting the curse and having a chance at a life had rejected her. Again.

Akari furiously swiped the rain and tears from her face with a sleeve. Why had she bothered to pursue him at all? Had she really expected anything different? She tried to tell herself she'd found the wrong man, but she couldn't deny the reflection of her own features and mannerisms that had answered the door. There was no question that he was her blood.

She hated him. Oh, she hated him!

The adrenaline fizzled, and her feet began to feel like they were shod with heavy earthenware pots. She stumbled over a gutter, caught herself on a bench, and sank onto it with a sob.

After several minutes of letting the downpour claim her, she glanced up. A man, somehow familiar, was approaching from across the street. He avoided meeting her eyes like a dog that knew it had done something to be ashamed of. She stood to leave as he came closer, but he held out a hand, his eyes lurching to meet hers.

Akari's breath hissed out in one incriminating syllable. "*You.*"

She sat down, her pulse quickening as indignation and disbelief tangled around each other in her chest. This was the same man she had confronted only a half hour ago, yet it seemed he had aged a year for each minute they had been apart. His hair was thinner, speckled with more white strands than black. The furrows between his eyebrows had spread channel-like creases that stretched across his entire forehead, and his pallor was like paper that had sat in the sun for too many years.

The man's forehead folds deepened. "I know I'm the last person you want to see, considering the meeting you just had with me." He rubbed a hand over his face and sighed. "But I've spent thirty years regretting this day. How you finally found me and I . . . I rejected you." His hand fell away, and he pinned her with his soul-sore expression. "I could not let one more day pass knowing I could have saved—" He winced. "I could have made a difference."

"But that was only moments ago." Akari wrapped her arms tightly around herself, as if by doing so she could keep her heart from unraveling. "You must have . . . did you board a timecraft to find *me*?"

She couldn't believe what she was asking. No one in her entire life had cared for her. She was the unwanted, after all, and it was fitting that trash should be discarded, forgotten in the streets. This had to be a mistake.

But the man nodded.

An incredulous frown pinched her brows together. Taking a time journey was incredibly expensive, not to mention risky. One could never predict how the most insignificant action could affect the future, and Saito Haru was a selfish, proud man—that's what she'd told herself her whole life. He would never risk such a reckless act.

The old man studied her a moment before kneeling on the wet pavement. "If I could have, I would have traveled back further than this to give you a childhood filled with opportunity instead of shame." His hands shook, and he wrung them together. "But this was as far as my wealth would allow."

Words became obstinate, reluctant to leave Akari's tongue. She stared at the man she had called many acidic things over the years. "Why—why did you do it? Leave a woman to have a child alone?" Her tears came in a hot torrent.

"And why wouldn't you claim me the first time I asked you?"

"When you were conceived, I was a coward. I thought a child would ruin my future, and I was already poor as it was. Then, when you found me again, I was accomplished and terrified that acknowledging my sins would ruin everything I had built for myself."

Akari bit her lip to stem the flow of anger. "And now?"

Saito Haru's mouth pulled into a hard grimace. "I refuse to abandon you a third time." He pulled a paper from his pocket, pressed it into her hands. "This is all I can give you," he whispered, reaching upward and gently resting his palms on her shoulders.

Staring down at the image of a lifeless body underneath the shocking headline, Akari felt sick. The corpse's face looked like hers, only far older.

This was her future.

She trembled under the man's touch.

"I name you Saito Akari. My daughter." A weak smile pressed through the sadness that defined his features.

The paper shimmered, then disappeared in her hands. Akari gasped when there was a sensation of something snapping from her chest like a cord being sliced free.

The *ichioyashide!*

She struggled to comprehend the gift he had given. A new life without the bane's magic constricting her, where she would finally be able to earn a living just like any other respectable member of society. It was all she had ever wanted.

But it wasn't supposed to happen like this. Surely, the cost was too great—the laws of time could not allow her father to walk free when he had cut such a gash in the fabric of time.

Even as she thought it, the broken man began to shine like the sun's glint on the twin oceans.

"*Oto-san!*" she yelped, grasping for his shirt but clutching only air. "Father!"

He evaporated into the rain, particle by particle until only his tear-streaked face remained. "I love you, Akari, and I should have a lifetime ago," he whispered.

He was gone.

Freedom. Gratitude. Astounding grief. Saito Akari tasted all three in the rain that fell on her lips.

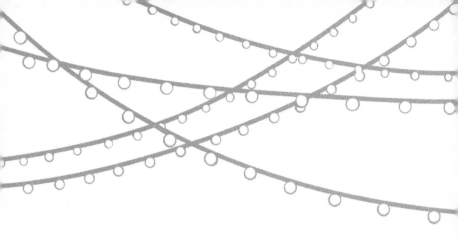

TO THE CHILD WHO
NEEDS TO HEAR IT

ALI NOËL

I'll climb the tallest tower
Swim the deepest sea
I'll slay a thousand dragons
to bring you back to me

I'll scare off every monster
Check the closet every night
I'll spin you fairytales
to help your dreams take flight

I'll listen when you're angry
Show you that I care
I'll say sorry when I've hurt you
to heal and repair

I'll remind you that you're worth it
Encourage, love and play
I'll support your gifts and passions
to keep your doubts at bay

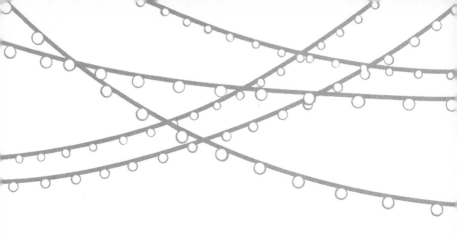

SOMEDAY

ANNE J. HILL

Someday, Harper would leave this place.

She hiked up her nightgown and lowered her tired body against the wall to guard the entryway. Some of the children were prone to sleepwalking, and the last thing she wanted was for them to wander the streets of Silverton in the middle of the night.

The door loomed in front of her—both a protection and a restraint from the world beyond. She had never been outside the kingdom of Conwell, not even out of Silverton, the small town mere miles from the sea. She closed her eyes and imagined stowing away on the steam engine that passed through town every week. Jumping off at the dock and boarding a pirate ship to take her far, far away from here.

Harper pulled the worn blanket over her lap and looked back to the door. That dream would never awaken. The orphanage was all she had known since she was three years old. And now, twenty years later, she was still unwanted. That nightmare was not about to change. When she was only sixteen, she transitioned from being under the orphanage's care to helping with the children in exchange for a place to live. Ms. Weatherbeard, the lady who ran the place, had dumped most of the less-loved duties onto Harper.

But it was a roof over her head.

"Miss Remming?" a tired voice spoke behind her.

Harper flinched and tore her eyes from the door. She forced a smile at the young boy. "Yes, Reed?"

His arms wrapped around his blanket, his bare toes wiggling on the cold floor. "I can't sleep."

Harper held her hand out to him. "What's the matter?"

He shuffled over and snuggled into her side. "Nightmares." His voice muffled against her. "Alla was telling me scary stories." His little fingers tightened around a fistful of her nightgown.

Harper thought for a moment, straightening his curls between her fingers. She could have left years ago, but besides her desperate need for a home, caring for these hurting children tethered her here. "Maybe if you tell me what's scary, then we can rationalize it."

Reed frowned. "What's *rat-on-a-liz*?"

Harper chuckled. "No, ration-a-lize. It means, well, that we can figure out why the stories aren't real and how they won't hurt you. Yeah?"

Reed bit his lip, his face scrunching in thought. "Okay." He took a deep breath. "She told me there's this place not far from here. A big manor, and it's haunted. Sometimes, ghost children leave there and go after other kids, trying to bring them into the manor." His small frame shivered.

Harper's fingers froze in his hair for a moment. "Did this place have a name?"

"Brimwood Manor."

Harper kissed the top of his head. "Well, Reed. I happen to know that none of that is true. Those are old wives' tales. Did you know that every year at Brimwood, the duke throws a huge party? All the nobles and rich people nearby go? And everyone, even the children, returns home unharmed? Sometimes, people like to make up stories about things they don't understand. Brimwood is only an old building, built long before we even had steam engines. But just because something is aged does not mean that it is haunted. So you have nothing to worry about."

Reed nuzzled his face against her. "But what if it *is* true?"

Harper smiled. "Then they'll have to get past me first. No one hurts Reed while I'm here."

He tilted his head back to beam hopefully at her. For a moment, they locked eyes, and Harper's chest seized.

"What about"—the smile on Reed's face faltered—"when you leave?"

The moonlight cast shadows through the window beside the door. Light and darkness swirled around the path to freedom.

Everything in her wanted to promise that she would never leave the little boy, that he could call her mother. But she knew broken promises were worse than no promises at all. She patted his head. "I'm here now, aren't I? Besides, I happen to know of a great pirate who can stare any ghost in the face and tell it to go away."

His eyes widened. "You do? Who?"

"You know him very well, too. He's fearsome and brave, and no ghost will overpower him. His name is Reed of Silverton, the Conqueror of the Seas." Harper ruffled his hair.

Reed's shoulders slumped. "I'm not a pirate. I'm just a boy."

She gasped dramatically and caught Reed's face in her hands. "*Just* a boy? No, you, little sir, are a brave boy. And the next time a nightmare tries to scare you, you lift your cutlass, stomp your foot, and tell it to go away."

"And what if it doesn't?" He sniffed.

Harper brushed her thumb over his nose. "Then you tell it again. You tell it that it's not allowed to live inside your head anymore. Because only light is allowed in. And if it still attacks you, then you go to war with it. Cutlass in hand, you fight. And you never stop fighting until the darkness is nothing but a shadow."

Reed took a deep breath. "Like a pirate would."

"Exactly like a pirate would. Reed of Silverton, the Conqueror of the Seas," Harper said. "Now. Sir Pirate, do you think you can try to sleep?"

"Can I sleep here with you, Miss Remming?" The moonlight from the window reflected in his eyes.

"Of course you can."

Harper lowered him down and watched the front door as he drifted off to sleep to fight his darkness.

Someday, Harper would leave this place. She would fight for the life that no one else had given her. And then, she would return and give that life to another.

Until then, she would raise her cutlass and scare away the nightmares.

The Brimwood Chronicles *is a fantasy series geared toward adult readers, set in Nathal, and will be published sometime in the next several years.*

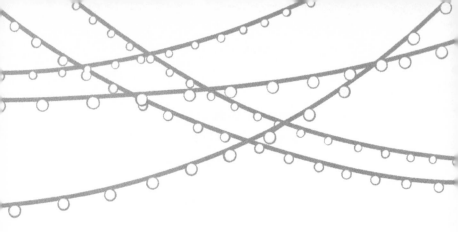

A PLACE
TO CALL HOME

NATHANIEL LUSCOMBE

There is a moment of unknowing
when strangers meet strangers.

The child can't look them in the eye.
He has dreamt of this for far too long,
worrying he will soon wake up.
He does not yet know of the open doors
in their homes and their hearts,
begging for him to pass through.

Breathless anticipation as he waits
until they finally begin to speak.
The reality sets in; he is wanted.

And if he is wanted, he must be loved.
He accepts when they invite him
to become part of their family.

There is joy on their faces and
joy in his soul as he realizes he has
a place to call home.

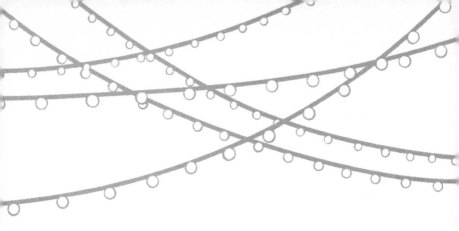

A HOME FOR NOVA

HANNAH CARTER
2022 Realm Award Flash Fiction Winner

Nova curled her legs up and tucked her toes underneath her nightgown. Damp tears rolled down her face as she sat on her bed in the dark. The curtains were drawn, and the mirror was covered up, as always, but even that couldn't blot out the reminder of her *differentness*, especially after today's latest incident.

She sniffled. No family wanted a freak. No home had room for someone so weird.

Nova's ear twitched, her thoughts interrupted by whispers wafting up through the air vent.

"The girl is an oddity," Miss Daisy said. "I'm quite unsure

why you would want her. She's been here eight years, and she scares away everyone. Besides, with this blasted foe war going on, we've got more orphans than we know what to do with. Certainly, you could find a more suitable child."

A deep, unfamiliar voice answered. "I enjoy a challenge." The person almost sounded amused.

"She's—"

"Miss Daisy, if you wouldn't mind, I'd like to see the girl now."

Nova squeaked and darted below her covers. Her heart hammered as she squeezed her eyes shut. Maybe if she could just disappear into the linens. Maybe if she could just fade away, like a moonbeam when a cloud snuffs out its light.

Her body trembled as the footsteps approached.

"I'd like to go in alone. I think the child might be more responsive that way," the masculine voice said.

"But—"

"I'll see you downstairs."

Miss Daisy spluttered out a few more warnings before she retreated. Nova clenched the thin sheets tighter and willed her visitor to vanish.

"Knock, knock." The man rapped once on the door as he announced his presence. The door creaked open. "Oh, dear. Is no one home?"

No one could see her in the dark. No lamp, no moon, no reflection. Nova had to be safe. He would leave soon.

The bed shifted as the man sat down on the edge. "Don't

tell Miss Daisy, but I smuggled in some contraband. Maple syrup bites."

Nova heard a soft crackling. "Mm. Delicious." His words slurred slightly. "And I've got a few out here to share with a certain someone if she'd come out of the covers."

Nova squeaked, which only made the stranger chuckle. "Ah, so she *is* there, quiet as a mouse." He adjusted his weight. "Come out, little mouse. I don't bite, even if it looks like I do."

She lowered the covers to her nose. A dark cloak disguised his features, even to Nova's keen eyes.

"Now, if you'll offer your name, I'll give you a sweet."

"N—Nova."

"What a pretty name." He held out his hand. Nova snatched up the treat and stuffed it in her mouth. "My name is Aster. Now . . . why are you locked up here in the attic?"

Nova's words were garbled as she chewed. "No one wants to room with me. They're all scared."

Aster clucked his tongue. "Oh, dear." He tucked his hands back into his mantle. "That's a shame. I took you for a rather nice girl."

Nova finally swallowed and nodded. "I try to be."

"I thought so. Say . . ." He leaned in close. "What happened to your ear?"

Nova reached up for the bandage that covered the tip. "In sewing class today, Melota snipped off the top with her shears. Said she was trying to make me *normal* because I'm a freak."

"Well, that's just awful. Why don't you let me check your

injury? I just need some light to see." Aster stood up and strode over to the dingy gray curtains.

As he grasped both ends, she lunged out of bed and fell flat on her stomach. "No! Don't open that!"

"Don't fear the moonlight, little mouse. Its beauty reveals your own."

Nova cried and stretched forward her hand to stop him, but it was too late. Aster parted the curtains, and the full moon shattered the dark.

Nova wailed and threw her arms across her face.

"Little mouse, look." Aster pried her arms away. "Don't be afraid anymore. You're not a freak."

Nova whimpered, but curiosity overrode her fear. She opened her eyes.

"See?" Aster's cloak tumbled to the ground as he spread his arms wide. His amethyst skin shone brightly. Just like hers. His white hair also seemed to glow, while pinpricks of light, which resembled the stars themselves, shimmered across his face. "Or am I a freak as well?"

Nova stared. Her large, black eyes, angular chin, pointed ears, and sharp nose—all of her unique features were mirrored on him.

She pressed her four-fingered hand against his forearm but yanked away quickly, embarrassed by her own impudence. But it was true; he wasn't a dream. Her lips quivered as she sucked in spasmodic breaths.

"You are a moon elf, little mouse." Aster smiled. "I've

spent years tracking missing children after the fae kidnapped thousands at the beginning of this war. Still, you are the first I've found." He reached out for her milky hair, the same shade as his own. "You are no freak, and you are wanted. You are the hope of our people's future. We'll keep you safe and cherish you."

Tears filled her eyes. They twinkled like diamonds even as she wiped them away. "Really?"

"Really." Aster scooped her up and held her so that the moonlight could illuminate all of her, not a bit left darkened by shadows. Her skin radiated a dazzling purple, brighter than even the brightest celestial body in the night sky. "I'm here to take you home, beautiful Nova."

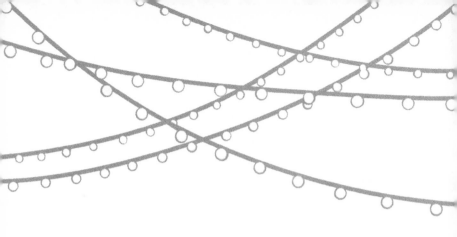

PALMS AND FOOTPRINTS

JADE LA GRANGE

As small as a song
Cradled within the core of a mountain,
As light as a river of sun
Streaming down grounds of barren dust,

There you were.

Wrapped in a blanket mold,
Little head peeking through the surface

There you were.

Eyes of sapphire blue,
Swimming in the sky above

Your fingers, small as spindles of a tree branch,
Strive for the heavens

And I'm completely enamored.

It's as though
You rise for me to raise you—
And raise you I shall,
Even though you're not of my bones.
I hold you in my arms,
Oh little babe of joy;
A covenant of blood I might not share with you,
But a covenant of home I surrender to you.

And while you're not strong enough to walk,
Let your feet
Pitter-patter on my heart,
Engraving footprints there.

And while you're grasping for something to grip,
Place your hands in mine;
Let them grip my fingers
And never let go.

You might be little, sweet child,
But your soul is mighty.
May I raise you to be nothing less;
May I raise you up
To Heaven itself,
That you may soar with wings like an eagle.

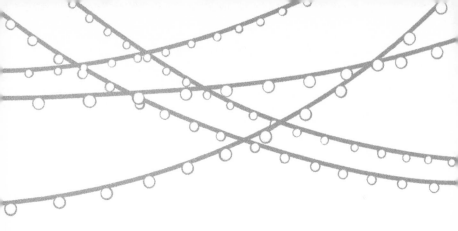

BUDGETING DAY

NATALIE NOEL TRUITT

Budgeting was Emma's least favorite chore. It only got worse when her two-year-old daughter lay on the floor in a tantrum because Emma had not let her play with a hammer. Now, Emma was trying to let her cry it out while she attempted to concentrate on arranging her expenses to make sense in her head. It was hard for her to focus on all of the numbers, and she was confident of only one thing—she was doing something wrong. She was six months out of high school and overwhelmed by the number of life skills she wished she had learned. Budgeting, taxes, how to iron a shirt. Since her own parents sucked, who was going to teach her these things?

A familiar *thump thump thump* hurried toward her, and she looked up. Margot crawled in her direction, sniffling and fussing. She held a light-up toy Emma had gotten from the Salvation Army that actually worked.

Emma sighed and picked her up. "What do you want, Margot Moo?" Margot waved the toy back and forth, and Emma blocked it from hitting her face. "I'm working on our budget. You know, so we can eat." Emma kissed the top of her head and breathed in the sweet scent of her curls.

Emma's saving grace was that she was going out with a friend the next day. Considering that she worked at a daycare where she could bring Margot with her, she could not remember the last time that she had a conversation with an adult. And the best part? Her friend's little sister would watch Margot for twenty dollars. After coffee, this would only be a thirty-dollar outing. Emma had been looking forward to it all week.

Emma rocked Margot back and forth, and she began to settle down. She babbled and sucked on her fingers. Emma kissed the top of her head again and took this as her cue to start working on her budget.

When Emma first started doing a budget, it was a lot of trial and error. There were some obvious aspects, such as rent and utilities, plus groceries and diapers. So, so many diapers. But she always felt like she was forgetting something.

As Emma finished the budget, she realized that, once again, she did not have any money left over to put into savings, and she was going to have to buy some packets of ramen to make sure that Margot could eat. She hated living paycheck to paycheck, but this was how it had to be for now.

Margot fussed, and Emma pushed down her frustration, resuming the gentle rocking. "What is it, baby?" She went through the normal checklist. Margot wasn't hungry. She shouldn't need a nap. Emma sniffed her bottom. Diaper change. She needed her diaper changed.

Emma took her to the changing table, humming softly. She pulled a diaper out of the pack and realized that there were only two left. She paused, her chest constricting. She felt nauseated.

She had another pack in her room, right?

Emma finished changing her baby, and then she went into her room and looked. She had been so sure that she hadn't needed to buy more diapers this paycheck, but a quick look at the apartment proved her wrong. The thirty dollars she had saved for going out with her friend disappeared from the budget, and she fought tears of frustration.

It was times like this that Emma wished that she had more support in her life, but she couldn't ask her parents. She could already hear the lecture. *Emma, you can't even afford to get baby diapers?*

She was alone.

She looked down at Margot. Margot smiled up at her.

Emma laughed, knowing that if she didn't laugh, she was going to cry. "Temperamental baby. Can I text my friend to say that I have to cancel, or is that going to make you cry?" Margot often cried when Emma was on the phone, not willing to share the attention.

An hour later, Emma had Margot down for her nap, and she sat in front of the TV with her phone. She sent her friend a text. **I have to cancel. Short on finances. Sorry!**

Deep-rooted shame and isolation filled her, and she curled up on the couch, ready to get lost in a true-crime series while her baby slept. Halfway through the episode, her friend responded. **No problem, but do you want to just go to the library instead? I'll get us coffee, and we can catch up while Margot plays!**

Something in Emma unraveled. She hadn't gotten help from her parents, but maybe that existed in other places. She responded. **Margot and I will see you Saturday!**

Emma leaned back against the couch and sighed with relief. For the first time in a while, she didn't feel alone.

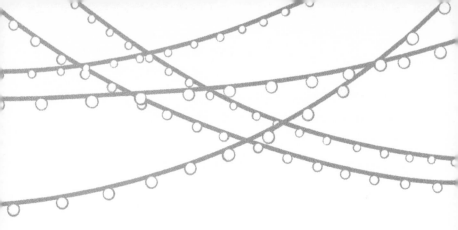

THIS LITTLE TABLE

SHANA BURCHARD

This little table is broken
But it does not matter to us—
For we have seen broken things
Made beautiful by the cross.

We break our bread here
And clasp our hands;
We bind each others' sores.

Through tender prayers
And steadfast love,
We open broken doors.

Yes, our little hands are broken,
But our past matters not.
For when we are together,
We are holding each others' knot.

We break our bread here
And clasp our hands;
We bind each others' sores.

Through tender prayers
And steadfast love,
We open broken doors.

We are infinitely tied together
By cords of scarlet blood
That poured out in victory
The day Christ showed us love.

We break our bread here
And clasp our hands;
We bind each others' sores

Through tender prayers
And steadfast love,
Lord, you have opened broken doors.

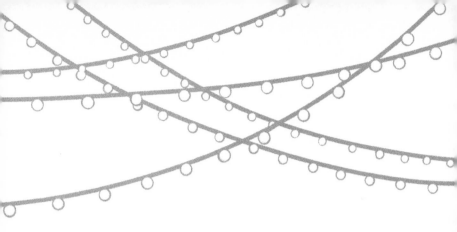

PRECIOUS CARGO

MORGAN J. MANNS

Sef!" I scream into the com. "Check your six!"

Three Darkbringer ships appear overhead. I watch from my cockpit as they close in on Sef. I flip a switch, boosting power to the defense shields, hoping he does the same.

As the black vessels fly in a triangular formation toward him, I wince, expecting their red laser blasts. But nothing happens. In less than a second the warships have bypassed him, already disappearing into the inky darkness, lost to the speckling of distant stars.

I exhale sharply. That was close. Too close.

Sef's gruff voice comes through the radio. "Why didn't

they shoot?"

I glance at my scanner screen. "Dunno. And why didn't we see them on the sensors?"

After a short pause, he says, "Maybe new cloaking technology? Whatever it is, thank the heavens they decided to spare us."

I turn to the bundle of linens behind me. Tiny fingers poke out of the swaddling as a contented coo reaches my ears. I can't help but smile. "Thank heaven, indeed. He's awake. Will you watch the skies for me?"

"'Course, Kip."

As the transmission ends, I unbuckle and step around my pilot's chair, reaching into the makeshift crib—a wooden crate, adorned with the few blankets I have onboard. As a man in my twenties, I didn't think to pack many comforts. A worn picture of my radiant wife, readily available coffee, and a couple of clean shirts is all I thought I needed. As I stare down at the babe, I wish I had more to offer.

"Did all that racket wake you up, little one? Don't worry, I've got you."

The babe's striking blue eyes, which Earth 6 is known for, gaze into my brown. He reaches out, babbling.

"You sure know how to tell a good story," I say, bringing my face closer. "You're the best co-pilot I've had in a long time."

He raises his small legs toward his chest and begins kicking them joyfully. How can such a little soul be such an uplifting presence? I extend my hand to meet his, my grin widening, and five perfect little fingers wrap around my thumb. The interaction sparks something within me, and a flurry of unexpected emotions strikes my heart faster than I can stop them.

My wife is due to give birth any day now, and I won't be there. Tears blur my vision as Kayte's radiant smile floods my thoughts. The memory of her sharing the news of her pregnancy through a distant video call, both of us brimming with excitement, is etched in my mind. The urge I had to leap through that screen just to hold her in my arms was overpowering.

My work in this distant part of the galaxy is important for the Resistance, yet my stomach twists with conflict. While I am committed to what we are doing out here, I can't shake the haunting feeling that, in choosing this path, I'm inadvertently failing my own family. I know it's the best choice for our planet's future, but I want nothing more than to be with my wife and soon-to-be-born son. Why is nothing in life easy? Every choice comes with a consequence.

The little one pulls his fingers away, begins to fuss, and tugs at the white linens wrapped around him. My attention draws back to him. He's ready to be picked up, it seems. As I begin to unwrap him from his bed, I remind myself that if I hadn't been on Earth 6 when the fighting erupted, this little one might not have survived. That, in itself, cements my belief that I have made a difference out here. I was meant to be on that planet.

Yet, the fact that his parents were killed during a Darkbringer attack while I was dropping off supplies on behalf of the Resistance still plagues my thoughts.

The memory sweeps over me. As I was unloading the water and food from my transport ship into a hospital, a fly-by bomber lit up the city with airborne explosives. When I found the crying babe—this babe—amongst the rubble, something pulled at my heart. I knew I couldn't leave him in that war-torn place. With his community in ruin and his parents dead, their people all but begged me to take him to safety.

How could I refuse?

Pushing the emotional memories away, I scoop him into my arms and find myself smiling again as he giggles. "I'm taking you to Earth 4, little buddy. Far outside the senseless fighting happening here. You'll be safe. I promise." I flick away a tear before it can fall on his perfect features.

Sef's voice cuts through my thoughts. "They're back! Brace yourself, Kip."

I hold the baby close to my chest and spin toward the cock-pit. The Darkbringer ships zoom past but still don't register on my sensors. Something else does, though.

"They've got a wurm following them," Sef announces, voicing my thoughts aloud.

I groan. It's their newest tactic. I should have seen it coming. Darkbringer ships seek out the humongous creatures and lure them to their enemies to do their dirty work for them.

It's a reckless and almost suicidal strategy, but one they're using more frequently. Perhaps a sign that the Resistance is successfully preventing them from obtaining more firepower for their ships.

"Can we outrun one?" I ask, slipping back into my seat with the baby still held close. Wurms are known to be fast, but I've never encountered one before. "I'm not sure if my cargo ship is cut for the job." The thought has my heart working double speed.

"Transfer the power from your shields to your engines, and we may have a chance. Just don't do it all at once. The inertial dampers can only handle so much. Gotta protect that baby."

"Roger, that. Sef." He's right. The babe won't be able to withstand any sudden acceleration. I'll have to do this gradually.

With one hand, I slowly send power to my engines, turning us toward the coordinates Sef has already sent me. The babe reaches out towards the blinking lights on the control panel, curious with wonder. I lean back so his little hands stay out of reach.

"You sure about this route?" I ask as I flick the next switch.

"If this wurm follows us, it'll be a challenge for the beast. It might prefer to double back on the Darkbringers instead."

Sef's confidence is comforting, but a sudden motion on the sensors draws my attention. I see the wurm change its course toward us. My pulse still hammers in my ears. It made its choice and abandoned its pursuit of the Darkbringers in favor of a slower meal.

Predictable but still terrifying.

As I peer into the inky void ahead of me, I see distant shapes come into view—massive rocks tumbling through space—the asteroid belt Sef wants us to hide in. It will either be our sanctuary or our graveyard. I swallow, hoping it's not the latter.

As the baby squirms in my arms, unaware of the looming danger, I offer a reassuring smile. He coos with delight. Glancing back to the dense rocks tumbling through space, I cling to Sef's hope that the snaking creature with coils of sleek, seemingly unending scales rippling down its gargantuan body, might reconsider hunting us through asteroids and opt for something else to devour. Goosebumps rise upon my flesh. I need to get this child to safety.

The baby gives up on reaching for the controls and begins a new game of pulling at the badges on my uniform. I plant a quick kiss on his brow. This baby deserves a chance at a full life.

After a quick discussion with Sef, we decide his ship should enter the asteroid belt first. With his vast experience, he'll find a path through.

I'm not proud enough to admit that Sef is the better flier out of the two of us. I've flown with him for only two short weeks, but it only took me a day to see that his skills far outweigh my own. How he instinctively knows exactly what to do in any situation is uncanny. He was born to live among the stars.

He's only a few years older than me but has years more piloting experience. He joined the Resistance at the ripe age of sixteen. Lied about his age, apparently. Forged the documents himself after his family was taken in a planetary raid by an early Darkbringer attack. Once the Resistance leaders figured out he was younger than he claimed, well, it was too late. He'd turned eighteen, rescued his own family in a daring solo mission and was too great an asset to punish. They awarded him a dozen medals and sent him on his way.

Sef was a legend among the Resistance and was now assigned to guard me as I returned home. It worked out well, seeing as he's supposed to pick up a new assignment once he reaches Earth 2, our home. If we survive this, I'll miss flying with him. I've learned more from him than any other flying instructor I've ever had.

I watch his ship carefully as it maneuvers perfectly between the first set of massive asteroids. My mouth goes dry as I realize I'm about to do exactly what he did.

"Keep your eyes on a swivel, Kip. The smaller rocks will disintegrate on your shields, but the larger ones sometimes collide, sending them on a new trajectory. Avoid them if you can."

I swallow. Fear grips me tighter than the controls in my hand. Driving through asteroid belts isn't exactly easy. There's a reason pilots avoid them. Autopilot won't help me here. With the broken rocks hurtling through space, unreadable on the sensors, I'll need to do this with my own hands.

My grip on the controls tightens, but one hand remains occupied, cradling the baby nestled within my arms. I won't risk putting him down. A cry from him could distract me at the worst possible moment. And I feel better knowing he's right here with me.

I maneuver past the first rotating rocks, all while sweeping my eyes from the sensors to the space around us. The wurm continues its advance, closing in. A sliver of terror snakes down my spine. It's fast. And so far seems undeterred by the onset of asteroids.

Sweat beads across my brow.

Sef's ship lies ahead, a guiding light through the darkness. I'm glad he was assigned to protect me on my way home with this precious cargo. Just having his presence is enough to settle my nerves.

I chance another glance down at the babe in my arms. He's fallen back asleep and his chest rises and falls in a steady rhythm. My heartbeat slows some. "We're going to get through this," I murmur, perhaps saying it more for my benefit than his.

"That wurm is gaining on us too quickly," Sef says factually. "We need to take a chance through the denser path."

I glance at the new coordinates and inhale a shaky breath. That is going to be some tricky piloting. The asteroids are in close clusters, leaving only a few ship lengths between each one. The path through will be like a minefield.

I focus on breathing steadily. "You know what you're doing. I trust you, Sef."

As we drive deeper into the belt, the asteroids close in on all sides. I'm constantly on the lookout for a stray rock, all while keeping my eyes on Sef. I don't want to lose him in here. The beeps on my scanner remind me the wurm is closing in. Sweat beads across my brow. It's going to chase us through this.

Just when I feel I'm getting the hang of driving through the asteroids, a group of shadows silently explodes above me. My eyes dart upward through the cockpit window. Two asteroids have collided, sending a flurry of smaller rocks tumbling outward in all directions. I wince, instinctually steering down through a clear path below me.

So much for following Sef.

The shards of rocks catch up quicker than I can risk accelerating with a babe in my arms. The sensors start ringing, alerting me to the rock's impact on my shields.

I hear Kip's voice on the com, but I barely register what he's saying. Something about watching behind me? I clench my teeth at the jarring movements. I don't need any reminders that the rocks are trying to blow open my ship, thanks.

I clutch the babe close. How is he sleeping through all of this?

Then, a huge impact knocks my ship forward, and

everything becomes a blur. I somehow wrap my body around the baby and wrench myself sideways, protecting his small form as I slam into the controls. He wakes up wailing, and my eyes flood over. Is he okay? Is he hurt?

Finally, the asteroid particles seem to have dissipated their assault on my ship. I don't feel their constant beratement into my shields anymore. No other impacts come.

As I search him over, finding no injuries, I breathe out a shaky sigh of relief. Was that one of the newly broken-apart asteroids that clipped us just now? It doesn't matter; I need to take a damage assessment of the ship if I hope to get us out of here in one piece.

Sensors and buzzers scream around me, and I struggle to get up to my knees. I don't think I broke anything, but my side is on fire with pain.

"It's okay. We're okay," I assure him and myself. But are we?

Ignoring the pain in my side, I take a quick inventory of the ship, noting the significant damage to the rear shields.

Sef's voice rings through the alarms. "Kip! Behind you!"

I grind my teeth, bracing myself, frustrated at not being able to catch my breath. Another asteroid? The babe still wails in my arms, adding to the deafening noise in my ears from the alarms. I can't focus.

Another impact rocks the ship and I clutch the babe close, wrapping my whole body around him. The ship is sent into a spin and I fall to the floor with him, pressed against the control panel, helpless to the rotations. I feel smaller asteroids slam into us and it's all I can do to hold him to my chest.

I have to get us out of this. I force myself to think, glancing at the control panel. The automated stabilizers must be down because we aren't slowing in our spin. If I can reach up and manually set the thrusters to get us straightened out . . .

The force of the spin makes it difficult for me to reach up my hand. But somehow, I do exactly that, and I'm able to flick the right switches and redirect power to the thrusters. They're still functioning. I let my hand drop, immediately feeling the change as the force gradually lessons and we begin flying in a straight trajectory.

I realize the babe is silent, even as the alarms continue their assault on my ears. Fear bleeds through me as I look down at him. His eyes are closed. *No!* I think, desperately. *He has to be okay.* I notice the rise and fall of his chest and my heart begins to beat again. I tuck him under my chin in relief and pray he hasn't suffered any trauma. That spin couldn't have been easy on such a small body.

Movement through the cockpit window catches my eye— a colossal maw resembling a cavernous abyss hurtles towards us, becoming larger with every second. Smaller asteroids bounce off its trailing serpentine form as the monstrous wurm comes for the finishing blow. I realize then that it's been battering us around like its own personal plaything.

I should be scared. Perhaps I am, but instead anger courses through me, drowning out everything else. I will not let this monster destroy this baby. Not after he's come so far.

I examine my control panel again, my brow creasing. This is a cargo ship. I don't have top-of-the-line weapons, but I have to at least try to use what I do have.

Adjusting the ship's thrusters, I position the vessel, aligning with the creature. With a press of a never-used button, the blasters roar to life. My chest leaps with anticipation. The red light at the front of the ship flashes with an unsteady rhythm. I've never used these blasters. I'm not certain how they'll fare against a beast of this size.

The red beam finds a steady rhythm and flares brighter than the sun. I can barely see the menacing wurm through the glaring light. Before the beam is able to slice away from the ship, it simply falters out, leaving me in sudden darkness.

No.

I panic, pressing the button repeatedly, but the ship is no longer responding. None of my blasters are working. My stomach churns as I realize I'm defenseless. The impacts the ship suffered must have damaged the blasters.

The wurm continues its advance. I shudder, tucking my head close to the babe's. "I'm sorry, little one. I've failed you." The words fall heavy on my tongue.

Then, a red blast flares toward the wurm, catching it in its side. At first, I think my own blaster has decided to work again, but then I see where the red blasts really came from. It's Sef, swooping in like a guardian angel amidst the chaos. His ship navigates the asteroid field, delivering a fusillade of red beams that assail the side of the wurm.

Immediately, the beast veers, targeting Sef. His lasers seem like more of an annoyance than destructive as they bounce of the wurm's armor like rain on a gutter. I swallow the boulder forming in my throat as I witness the inevitable collision.

"Kip, you get that babe to safety. It's been a pleasure flying with you."

Sef's words ring in my ears, and I gasp at his farewell. I realize then—he's sacrificing himself for us.

"Sef!" I scream, but it's too late.

The beast's gargantuan head collides with Sef's ship and it redirects the fighter into a massive asteroid, breaking the ship into pieces beyond recognition.

My mouth hangs open as the beast falters. I'm not entirely sure if it's stunned or dead. Sef on the other hand . . .

There's no question. He's gone. Dead.

I snap my mouth close, sniffing back the tears threatening to fall and narrow my gaze on the creature. Sef's sacrifice has to be for something. The beast drifts aimlessly, but its massive eyes seem to lock onto mine.

Under the weight of my furious whisper, "You vile beast!" I press the button that launches my blaster, eyes widening in disbelief as my ship responds with an unprecedented surge of power.

No flickering lights, just a swift gathering of energy at the helm. Holding my breath, a singular crimson beam slices through the darkness, aimed at the monstrous wurm.

A catastrophic eruption of red light engulfs the creature's eye, annihilating its head.

The sound of the alarms around me fade with my shock, leaving me suspended between relief and grief.

I lose a breath and muffle a sob, resting my cheek upon the babe's still-sleeping head. "It's done. We're safe now." The babe continues sleeping, undisturbed by my words.

There's no time to mourn Sef. As much as I want to drop to my knees and let the tears flow, this babe is my priority. If I can't get this ship through this asteroid field, I've left us for dead.

Wincing through the pain I feel in my side, I work at the ship to get it back into working order. Realizing I need two hands to fix the problems I find with the thruster responders, I place the sleeping babe back into his makeshift crib, checking on him every other minute.

He hasn't woken since that awful spin that monster put us into. I try not to think about what that means. He has to be okay.

Eventually, after more than an hour, I get the ship into a state where it'll fly. The alarms stop, and I slump into my chair, exhaustion catching up to me. The pain in my side still makes each breath I take difficult. I continue to ignore it, staring at the coordinates Sef left before he made that sacrifice.

I wipe away a stray tear. He's given us a probable path through the asteroids. It's still uncertain—asteroids are unpredictable, but it's the clearest one he's found.

I grip the controls and follow the path, feeling like Sef is still here, guiding us through.

After hours of tense flying, I emerge into clear black space. We've made it.

I press my head into my hands, letting the tears finally flow. I stay like that for God knows how long.

Sef's dead. The man who, in such a short time, taught me so much, and gave his life for a baby he doesn't even know.

Not only that, the Resistance has lost one of its top fighters. I'll need to tell his family what he did for us, for everyone . . .

A twinkling sound brings me out of my grief-stricken trance. Another alarm? No—wait, that's a video call. Someone's trying to contact me.

I blink away tears, steeling myself before tapping to accept the call. I expect one of the Resistance's captains is trying to reach me for a status report. I'll need to report Sef's death. I press the button.

Kayte's radiant face floods my screen, bringing tears to my eyes all over again. My beautiful wife. She's everything to me.

"Kip, I've been trying to call you for hours. Are you okay?"

I swallow, trying to mirror her smile. "I'm sorry, the asteroids must have been messing with my long-range video calling."

"Asteroids!?" Her smile dips into concern and she leans toward the screen.

I wince, wishing I hadn't worried her. I can't bring myself to tell her what I've been through. Not yet. Not when it's so fresh in my memory. I shake my head, waving a hand, hoping she brushes it off as a minor mishap. "Yes, but that doesn't matter now—How are *you*? I thought we weren't scheduled for a call until," I glance at Earth 2's date on the screen, "two days from now."

The wide-grinned smile returns to her face. "I thought it was important to tell you that our son was born."

My heart leaps in my chest. It's happened. She's given birth. My mouth falls open and I've lost my ability to speak.

"Let me introduce you to Jeffery Kiplan Skalsky." Kayte smiles and moves the camera away from herself, showing a very new baby boy sleeping peacefully against her chest.

My words catch in my throat as I lean forward, wishing I could jump through the screen to hold my family. Finally, I find my voice. "He's beautiful, and I . . . I think the name we chose for him suits him to a T."

A small cry brings me back to my present situation. At first I think it's Jeffery, but our son is still asleep against his mother's chest.

"Kip? I thought I heard a baby cry?"

It's my tiny co-pilot. "Just a moment, Kayte. This little one is awake, I think."

One of the last conversations I have with Sef rolls over me like a tidal wave. I think about how he did indeed watch the skies for us, doing everything he could to make sure I was able to make it through as a father and to help this little babe survive.

I scoop up the babe and my muscles relax as I realize he is okay. He smiles up at me, looking for the badges on my jacket he's so quickly come to enjoy playing with.

Bringing him back to the screen, I find myself smiling wide.

"Kayte, I've finally thought of a name that might suit *this* little one. Let me reintroduce you to Sef." I look into her eyes. "There's much to talk about, but perhaps he could be Jeffery's older brother?"

Kayte's eyes widen a little, but soon relax as she gazes down at Jeffrey. "You know what, Kip, that sounds like a wonderful idea. We always talked about adoption."

I know then, that Sef's legacy will live on.

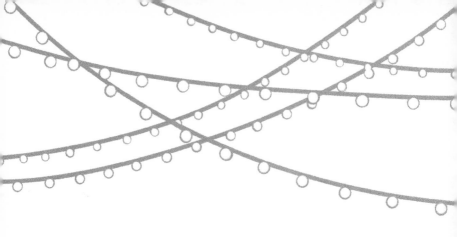

CHUBBY CHEEKS

ANNE J. HILL

As I held him in my arms
I wished I could bring him home
But that was not our story

For a brief moment of his life
I was able to play a role
from late-night bottles
to early-morning cuddles

I have no idea where
he calls home these days
but his little laugh
and chubby cheeks
still fill me with joy

And someday, perhaps
I'll be able to care for
a baby in need until they're grown
I did not have much desire for this
until I met him

I cling to our shared moments
the treasured memory of his smile
and I pray God keeps him
in His care until the end of his days

For now, I'll hold him in my heart
and pray he has a safe home
Someday I'll hear his full story

This poem is about a baby I cared for several years ago at one of the baby homes this book is supporting.

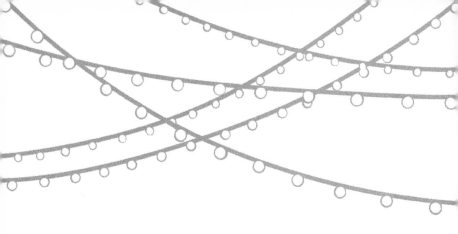

TO SAVE A STORY

H. L. DAVIS

Y ou may be twelve, but you are still the messiest of Sylvtír when you eat berries." Though Greta chided, she couldn't hide the twinkle in her eyes as she pointed a crooked finger toward the creek.

I smirked at the purple splotches on my hands, then over at my guardian. "If I must." I gave her a peck on the cheek and skipped away. Kind Greta. After all the years she'd taken care of me, the least I could do for her was wash off some berry juice.

I scrubbed my hands and splashed my face, the water's cool touch a relief after a hot afternoon of foraging. I glimpsed my reflection in the creek, frowning at how the verdant canopy above made my hair burn extra bright.

My strange red hair had led my own mother to abandon me at Greta's doorstep. Made other forest folk keep their distance as from an unruly flame. Most Sylvtír feared what they didn't know or understand. But, thank the Maker, Greta's heart was as large and golden as the sun.

A sound suddenly broke through my thoughts. Faint, but shrill as it wafted through the trees.

Crying?

I turned toward Greta, who sat nearby fanning herself with her hat, the open hamper of dewberries at her feet.

"Do you hear that?" I asked.

"Hear what, child?"

"That!" I darted in the direction of the noise. Greta rose with a grunt and hobbled after me.

Light filtered through the branches of firs and pines overhead, causing pale patches to mingle and dance among the shadows on the forest floor. I surveyed the woods I knew so well, searching for the source of the wails. My heart leaped when I spotted it: a large basket resting idly at the bole of an old oak. I raced to it, the cries growing louder as I knelt and lifted the lid.

A baby . . . A tiny baby, out here, all alone, with only a thin blanket for comfort! It squinted as the day's brightness struck its eyes—the silver eyes of a Sylvtír girl—trying to rub away the discomfort with a small fist.

"Well, I'll be." Greta came to a stop beside me, grinning so that all the gaps in her teeth were on display. "Ain't that a sweet sight." She set down her hamper once again, a couple of dewberries escaping in a roll across the mossy ground.

"What's she doing this deep in the forest? All by herself?"

Greta's smile faded. "Look closely, Aylee. I believe you'll find your answer."

I examined the little girl's face. Rich brown skin. Eyes shiny from weeping. Tiny mouth. Pale hair. And her ears—

"Her pointed ears?"

Greta nodded, a gloom clouding her normally cheerful countenance. "It's a legend as ancient as these woods that a babe who develops pointed ears isn't truly one of our kind at all, but a changeling left by the faeries to bring mischief and misery; the true Sylvtír, stolen away. All nonsense, if you ask me. But you know"—Greta placed a gentle hand on my shoulder—"how forest folk fret, holding fast to their tales."

Anger rose within me, blazing as red as my hair. "So pointed ears, too, mean a child is only worth abandoning?" I planted both fists on my hips. "That's wrong!"

The baby whimpered, her face scrunched in displeasure at my heated words. Concern dousing my vexation, I gently scooped her up in my arms and snuggled her close.

"If no one else will care for her, I will." My voice was resolute. "Just as you have done for me. I don't care what the forest folk say. I won't let the old tales take away her chance to live her story."

Greta's tan, wrinkled face beamed with pleasure. "Come then, my dears. Let's go home."

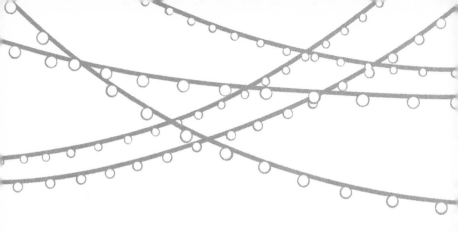

HEART OF THE INNOCENT

C. F. BARROWS

Come and hear now the tale
Of the child of a beggar-man—
How his world changed overnight,
And how all he held dear
Was ripped from his fingertips.
He tried to make it all right
For the one in his care.
All he had, even his life, he'd gladly spend
For one little boy
With the heart of an innocent.

The price of his soul
Seemed a small one to pay,
But the deal was only the start.
And the child of a beggar-man
Found that his means of escape
Had fallen apart.
But a desperate man, he holds tight to his plans;
He does things that he never meant.
And with one blow,
He shattered the heart of the innocent.

Well, the beggar-man's child,
His time came to an end.
So the little boy he left behind
Went searching for love,
Searching for light—
But darkness was all he could find.
Long he lived in the night;
It was all that he knew.
But something inside was still bent
On finding someone
To rebuild the heart of the innocent.

Though the darkness said
There was no light to be found,
The innocent searched, and then
He thought another would help

HEART OF THE INNOCENT

Mend the shards of his soul,
But they shattered him over again.
Oh, hear how he cries—
How his hope, now it dies;
How in fear
To the flames he went.
Now so black,
Black is the heart of the innocent.

Now the light burns his eyes,
And when love comes, he flies.
When he falls, no one sees his descent
But one girl,
One with the heart of an innocent.

Now the darkness abates
And the innocent waits,
Daring to trust once again.
Is there still hope,
Hope for the heart of the innocent?

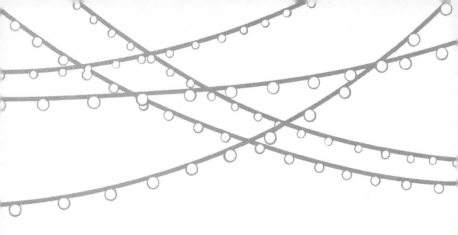

PORT IN A STORM

BROOKE J. KATZ

Even with the volume on Killian's iPod maxed out, the yelling in the other room clashes against Paul McCartney's vocals. He is an underrated bass player, in Killian's humble opinion. Squinting in concentration, he ghosts his fingers across the strings, pretending to play "Paperback Writer" by the Beatles on his own bass guitar. He is careful to not make a noise—he doesn't need the storm in the living room to whisk his way.

He hides in his room; the late afternoon sun is all he needs for light. The Gulf of Mexico glistens like an array of diamonds just beyond the condos on the other side of the street. Lost in the music, he startles when a bang against his door shakes the window. He takes out his earbuds. Several more bangs resound. He stays perfectly still, holding his breath. Maybe, if he is silent, she'll think he fell asleep and give up or forget he is even here.

"Leave him alone, Allie," his dad scolds her.

"I will not! He's my son, Steven, and we are leaving. You hear that, Killian? We are leaving. Pack your bags!" She almost sounds sober, but it's too late in the day for that to be true.

"Knock it off. You're probably scaring him." His dad sounds exhausted.

"Don't touch me! You like to play like you're the perfect parent, but you're not!"

Killian swallows the lump in his throat. He wants to slip the earbuds back in and disappear, but he needs to listen for her to go away so he can leave without confrontation.

Their unit is on the fifth floor, too high to escape out the window.

His parents' raised voices and harsh words escalate outside his door. His heart palpitations increase with each syllable. Needing to calm down before a full-blown panic attack kicks in, Killian breathes in through his nose and out through his mouth, as Aunt Ruth taught him, and with each breath, the voices fade further away from his door.

When he feels like it's safe to move, he gets up and packs his backpack with a few essentials. He places his bass guitar in its case and latches it closed as silently as possible, then presses his ear to the door. The bathroom door on the other side of the condo slams shut.

This is his chance.

Cracking the door, he peeks straight ahead at the mirrored wall next to the front door. He doesn't see his mom, just an empty dining room and living room.

Killian grabs his sandals from the closet by his room. Sand still lingers on the bottoms, leaving a little trail when he tiptoes to the front door and slowly pulls it open. It makes a suctioning noise, and his heart pounds hard in his chest.

He looks around, making sure his mom hasn't heard him. Hearing the sound of the shower running in his parents' bathroom, a sigh of relief escapes his lips. There's still time.

He hears the lanai's sliding glass door scrape open and then close.

Killian straightens. He catches his dad's reflection in the mirrored wall across from him. Dad walks around the white couch and leans against the back of it, facing Killian. He doesn't fear his dad or his response to him leaving. His dad will understand because Mom's episode is *bad* tonight.

"Are you heading to the McConvilles then?" His dad's voice is tired but tender.

"Yeah."

"You better go quickly." He walks around the corner, locking the door to Killian's room. "I'll tell her you're asleep."

Killian nods, and his dad walks toward him, engulfing Killian in his arms. "I love you, son . . ." He takes a deep breath, holding Killian by the shoulders to look him in the eyes. "I'm sorry."

Killian nods, blinking back his unshed tears. He gives his dad one more hug before he leaves.

"Tell McConville thank you for me . . . for everything."

"You can tell him yourself, Dad. Uncle Tom is your best friend."

His dad reaches for the door. "You better go, kiddo, before she comes back out. Love you." He tousles Killian's hair.

"Love you, too."

Now that Killian's fear has subsided and his other senses are coming into focus, he notices his dad's eyes are red, and he smells kind of like a skunk. He knows what his dad was doing out on the lanai now, and the disappointment sinks like a stone in his stomach. His dad gives him a nod.

"Be safe. It's getting dark. Have Uncle Tom or Aunt Ruth call when you get there."

"Yes, sir." Killian salutes him.

His dad laughs. It's something Killian has done since he was little, after the two of them watched *Major Payne* together.

Shutting the condo door behind him, Killian can finally breathe. He makes his way to the elevators. He should have stayed down at The Docks helping Mr. Daniels—owner of the island's marina—close up for the night. He hadn't thought it would get this bad until later, when it was bedtime and he could sleep through the storm.

When he turns toward the elevators, his sandals slap against cream tile. After pushing the elevator button, it doesn't take long for the doors to slide open. He steps in, met by his own haggard reflection in the mirrored walls. He looks tired, his dark brown waves swept out of his face, dark circles faintly noticeable against his olive skin. He's always been told that he takes after his mom, and the thought makes his stomach twist. She morphed into someone he doesn't recognize, someone he fears at night. She's never hit him, but her words and absence hurt just as bad.

His mom's drinking didn't used to be this bad—at least not from what he can remember.

At one point, they all used to be close, like a real family. Something shifted in his family that he still doesn't understand. Maybe his parents were always this way and he only noticed it as he got older, but all his mom has wanted to do since he was ten is party and drink. His dad used to join her, and they would leave Killian at Uncle Tom and Aunt Ruth's overnight and sometimes for whole weekends while they went out to party together.

Killian wishes he could be at the McConville's permanently. The McConvilles aren't his biological family, but they might as well be. Their daughter, Ennis, is his best friend, though over the years she's become more like a sister. Since neither have siblings of their own, they unofficially adopted each other. Even though his parents' relationship with the

McConvilles has suffered, Killian has only grown closer to them.

A jolt and ding lets Killian know he made it to ground level. He steps into the condo lobby. Keeping his head down, he pushes open the frosted glass doors that lead to freedom. He unlocks his bike from the bike rack, yanking it out of its spot, and sets off, balancing his bass in the middle while he expertly steers one-handed.

Thick, salty air suffocates him as he peddles out of the garage.

August in Florida is no joke. The lack of a breeze helps nothing. He follows the main road with the Gulf to his left and inland to his right. Red, pink, and orange hues paint the sky, casting the island in its own beautiful filter. El Mar, Florida, is his home. This small island town is a hidden gem, where the locals all know each other and the snowbirds visit each year, finding solace from the harsh northern winters.

Just a few more blocks and his port in a storm comes into view. The sky blue Victorian house sits on stilts that are hidden behind white lattice. Killian and Ennis have spent many evenings on the covered white wraparound porch reading or playing music with Uncle Tom while Aunt Ruth reads from her Bible, the metal from her porch swing creaking in time to their rhythm. It's always been his favorite part of staying with them. That porch is where Uncle Tom taught him to play bass, where he shared his most honest thoughts and feelings, where he met God. He'll never forget that night. He and Ennis were ten years old. Ennis was painting and Killian and Uncle Tom were playing checkers while Aunt Ruth read to them from the book of Ephesians. Chapter one, verse five hit him right in the chest as if it had been written just for him.

As he biked, Killian whispered the verse to himself. "God decided in advance to adopt us into his own family by bringing us to himself through Jesus Christ. This is what he wanted to do, and it gave him great pleasure."

When he found Jesus that day, he found the love and belonging he had been longing for. The more time he spent with the McConvilles, he experienced the love of Jesus and what it meant to have a true relationship with Him every day, not just on Sundays in church. Now, every night, Killian prays to live with the McConvilles permanently.

Seashell gravel crunches beneath his bike's tires when he pulls into the driveway. Hopping off his bike, he parks it beneath the carport beside the house.

The weather-worn steps creak beneath his weight, and he pulls out the braided string necklace hidden beneath his shirt. Ennis made it for him to hold the house key, a loving reminder that their home was always open to him. Humidity causes the swollen door to stick to the frame. He slams his shoulder into the door, and it jerks open. A gust of the cool AC greets him like a hug of relief.

"Killian lad! I thought that was you." Uncle Tom's lyrical accent reaches him. "Here, give me your bass. I'll go put it in your room." Uncle Tom's once black hair is peppered with more grays these days. A smile spreads across Killian's face as he makes himself at home.

"Thanks, Unc. Where's Ennis?" Killian kicks off his shoes and lines them up with the others, just as Aunt Ruth likes.

"She's in the living room getting her butt kicked in Monopoly."

Killian follows Uncle Tom through the house. Pictures line the walls, telling the story of how their families became connected. Uncle Tom and his dad stand in their caps and gowns for their college graduation. Killian and Ennis had heard the stories. Uncle Tom had come to Florida from Ireland to go to university. That was where he met Killian's dad in a study group, where they bonded over a mutual love of hurling.

Killian's favorite picture of the two of them is the one where they have their arms slung around each other and were caught laughing hard. Uncle Tom has frosting covering his face and Dad's holding the smashed-in birthday cake.

There are photos of Uncle Tom in front of his bookshop he opened shortly after graduation. Killian's dad, an architect, helped him design the layout, including the hidden garden in the back with mini book huts.

Uncle Tom and Killian's dad had remained best friends, and Killian's childhood was full of memories of the combined families. That is, until after Killian turned ten and everything began to change. At first, the shift was gradual, sleeping in and missing church, turning down outings with the McConvilles. His parents started leaving Killian with the McConvilles on weekdays and almost every weekend so they could go out with their "other friends."

Uncle Tom takes Killian's things to the upstairs guest room, which slowly morphed into Killian's space over the years. Posters of his favorite bands decorate the walls with pictures of him and Ennis with their friends. Killian heads into the living room. He smiles at Aunt Ruth and Ennis sitting on the floor around the coffee table.

"This game is stupid." Ennis scrunches her nose while handing Aunt Ruth the fake money.

"Don't be a sore loser." Aunt Ruth giggles at Ennis' pouting.

"Killi! Thank goodness you're here." Ennis trips on her way over to Killian and crashes into him.

"Oof. Hey, prawn." Killian picks her up in a bear hug and spins her around. "One foot in front of the other." He laughs, setting her down.

"You can help me beat these two at Monopoly. They're both cheaters." She glares over at her mom, who mouths "sore loser," placing an L shape with her fingers on her forehead.

Killian bites his lower lip to keep from laughing. Ennis rolls her eyes, crossing her arms.

"Ah, my little fairy, did you lose?" Uncle Tom comes back down, kissing Ennis on the forehead.

"How about we put the game away and have a movie

night?" Aunt Ruth starts putting away the pieces.

"I'll make the popcorn. Oh, and Killi, I'll call your Da and let him know you're here," Uncle Tom offers.

"Killi, you have to come see the painting I'm working on first." Ennis grabs his hand, pulling him toward the stairs. Killian climbs the stairs behind her, the anxiety from earlier falling away with each step he takes. It's good to be home.

Killian jerks awake; Ennis is shaking his shoulders. "Killi, wake up!"

"Ennis? What's wrong?"

"How can you sleep through this?"

"Sleep through what?" He props himself up on his elbow and rubs the sleep from his eyes.

She sits on the edge of his bed. Familiar voices work their way upstairs. He looks at Ennis. His mom and dad are downstairs. He can practically hear his heart beating in the silent room. He searches Ennis's eyes for what to do.

"I don't know what's going on, but Da is mad, Killi, really mad. I don't think I have ever heard him so mad before. He started swearing in Irish."

"At my dad?"

Ennis shakes her head. "At your mom. Your dad was yelling at her, too."

"Did you hear what they were talking about?"

"I think . . . I think my parents want you to live with us permanently."

Killian swallows. This is what he has been praying for, but he is too scared to let himself hope that it is finally coming true.

He looks at the clock, and the red numbers jump out at him. "It's the middle of the night! En, what happened?"

"It's your mom. That's what woke me up. She was screaming at Da that you're hers and she's a good mom, blah blah blah."

Killian's heart sinks; words are his mom's weapon of choice.

"What should we do?"

"Let's just crack the door open and see if we can hear better. I think they are in the kitchen, though. It may be hard to hear."

The hinges creak and echo in the hallway. Killian holds his breath but lets it out in a whispered giggle when he sees Ennis has her eyes closed.

"Why are you closing your eyes, prawn? You think if you close your eyes, they won't hear the door?" She gives him a withering stare.

"Shut it, Killi." They both turn their ears to the opening. Killian whispers in her ear.

"I can't hear coherently. It's like listening to Charlie Brown's teacher yelling into the phone. Let's sneak down."

"Okay, let me go first." She slips out of the doorway with

Killian at her heels. The two of them creep downstairs as quietly as the creaky stairs allow.

Killian doubts anyone hears them over the screaming. They both sit in the dark, hidden, slouched in front of the couch. The yelling seems to have calmed down.

"Al, why don't you go home and get some rest? We can talk tomorrow." Ruth calmly suggests.

"Oh, shut it, Miss High-and-Mighty. You just want to steal my kid from me."

"Allison, stop, that's not what they are doing." Killian's dad firmly proclaims.

"Oh, you're in on it, troll."

"There will be no name-calling in my home." Tom is clearly done.

"I want my kid now!" his mom slurs.

"I'm not traumatizing our son. He is safe here. Now let's go home and sleep this off."

"I'm not a bad mom." She hiccups and sniffles.

"No one is saying that, Allison." Ruth's calming voice brings peace to the chaos. "We all know how much you love him."

Killian clenches his fist. How she shows love is not love at all.

"I'm tired. I'm going home. Let's go, Steven," his mom demands.

"No, Allison, you should not drive," Uncle Tom says.

"I drive jusss fine."

There's a scuffle.

"Give me the keys back, Allison." His dad's voice is stone cold.

"Fine! You want them?" Her voice is menacing.

There is a metallic thud, followed by a scraping across the floor. A clatter. His dad curses.

"You almost hit me!" his dad yells.

Footsteps stomp across the kitchen tile, and the door groans open and slams shut.

The kids hear a collective sigh in the kitchen, like everyone had been holding their breath.

"I'm sorry, Tom, Ruthie. I'm so sorry I brought her over, but she was so insistent and I didn't want her driving. I don't know what to do anymore. I can't leave her, but my son is not safe at home. I'm worried about him. His grades are slipping. He isn't himself . . ." More scraping against the floor, like someone righted a chair.

Killian takes a deep breath. This is his cue to go in. He pushes to his feet. Ennis follows him.

"Dad?"

The adults snap their heads in the kids' direction.

"I suppose that woke you two up. Didn't it?" Ruth asks.

Both kids nod.

"Steve, you're my best mate," Uncle Tom says. "Your son is like my own flesh and blood. You know I will do whatever to help you and him. Allie needs help, and Killi is getting caught in the crossfire. But I never want you to feel we are trying to take him from you."

"Tom, I have never thought that. Not ever."

"Dad?" Killian tries again.

"Yeah, son?"

"I don't want to go back to the condo. It's not that I don't love . . . I mean . . . I want to stay here with the McConvilles. It feels . . . It . . ." He struggles to say it out loud.

"You feel safe here," his dad says it for him.

Killian lowers his head; he doesn't want to hurt his dad or his mom.

"Killian, I understand. Don't worry. You don't have to come back tonight, and you can stay as long as you want." His dad grips the back of the chair he must have picked up. "I better go make sure your mom gets home safe."

"Are you okay to drive?" Aunt Ruth asks.

"Yeah, Ruthie, I haven't had a single drop tonight." Killian's dad reaches the door. "Good night, you guys."

Once the door closes, Killian sinks to the kitchen floor. His face feels wet and his chest constricts. He can't breathe. He holds his fists to his stomach, squeezing his eyes shut. Uncle Tom, Aunt Ruth, and Ennis join him on the cool tile. They hold him for as long as he cries.

"Father, we pray for Killian," Uncle Tom starts. "Lord, keep him safe and give his mum and da the help they need. Help us to care for him and give him a home where he feels safe and loved. Lord, in You we trust to help us all through this, giving You the glory all the way. In Jesus's name, I pray, amen."

Killian's chest releases. The tension in his hands and stomach relaxes its vice grip. He breathes in through his nose and out through his lips. He doesn't have to leave.

It's only been one week, and this already feels like home, Killian thinks with a smile as they pull into the driveway after church. His dad, who looks worse than the last time Killian saw him, sits waiting on the porch steps. His dad stands up awkwardly, brushing invisible dirt from his pants. The McConvilles give his dad quick hellos and hugs before going inside to give them some privacy.

"Hey, son, I wanted to bring over some more of your things. Are you doing well?"

Killian takes the suitcase. "Yeah, Dad, I'm doing good. Thanks for bringing more of my things over."

His dad shoves his hands in his pockets. "Good. I miss you, kid." He pulls his hands out and quickly hugs Killian. "I better get back home. Love you, kiddo."

"Yeah, sure, love you too, Dad. Thanks again." He watches his dad descend the steps and slide into his beat up Ford truck and take off. Killian doesn't dwell on the awkwardness; he bounces up the stairs to get ready to go windsurfing with Ennis.

"You know what, prawn?" Killian questions Ennis. They take a break on the shore between waves. Killian hands her one of the sandwiches Aunt Ruth packed them. She takes it, handing him his water bottle.

"What?" She doesn't look up from her task of unwrapping the cling wrap from her sandwich.

"You're getting pretty good at windsurfing, and the perk of you being so short is you can still use a kiddie-size board, saving us money on rental fees." She stops her unwrapping task long enough to playfully shove him. Killian laughs.

"Ow, hey now, what are brothers for?" Killian laughs before taking a bite of his sandwich. Ennis balls up the cling wrap, and he takes it from her to put back in the cooler.

"I may be short, but I'm speedy."

"True. You have really gained confidence out there on the water."

"Thanks, Killi. I had some pretty okay teachers this summer with you and Fitz." She nudges him with her shoulder."

"Just okay? I'm insulted." He smirks at her, and she rolls her eyes, taking a sip of water.

"Mmm!" Ennis quickly swallows her water, her eyes wide and face turning serious. "Hey, I kind of saw some official looking papers at Da's bookstore the other day. I couldn't really get a good look, but some of them had your name on it with your dad's signature and your mom's."

"Could you imagine, En, we could actually be siblings."

"We already are siblings, butthead. I don't need a piece of paper to say that."

Killian's attention is stolen by Mr. Daniels walking toward them from The Docks. His Hawaiian shirt flaps open, exposing the white tank underneath.

"Hey, Mr. Daniels." Ennis gives him a hug.

His smile puts Killian at ease instantly. "Just the two I was looking for."

"What can we do for you?"

"Actually, your folks are looking for you two. Ennis, your da just rang and said to come to the house immediately."

"Sounds serious." Killian hopes he doesn't have to go back to the condo.

Ennis starts packing up their things.

Fear grips Killian in a paralyzing chokehold. Mr. Daniels puts his hand on Killian's shoulder. "Whatever it is, Killian, God will see you through. Remember that."

"Yes, sir." Killian allows his encouragement to melt him from his frozen stupor.

"Do you two want a ride?" Mr. Daniels asks.

"No thank you, we have our bikes." Ennis speaks for both of them.

They pack their bags and the cooler in haste and make their way back to the parking lot. The beach is not crowded this afternoon, and they easily maneuver toward the bike racks.

Killian leans over, his hands fumbling with the lock on their bikes until it finally pops open. He stands and quickly mounts his bike, taking his helmet from Ennis's extended hand.

"Are you okay, Killi?" Ennis grabs the handle of his bike.

"I don't know, En . . . I'm scared."

"Whatever it is, I'm here with you."

He lifts his mouth in a tight smile.

"Thanks, En. Come on, let's get home quick." In spite of the sun's warm rays, Killian fears a storm may be brewing. *Jesus, I don't know what's going on, but whatever I'm walking into, be with me.*

Killian and Ennis sit dumbfounded at the kitchen table. Aunt Ruth stares at her clasped hands. Uncle Tom clears his throat and shifts in his seat. He looks outside to the swaying hibiscus.

"Killi?" Aunt Ruth brushes the back of his hand to get his attention. "Are you going to be okay, sweetheart?"

Is he going to be okay? This is what he wanted, isn't it? To live here, to be adopted by his favorite people? Then why is part of him hurting so much?

"So wait a minute, let me sum this up: Mom and Dad were both under some sort of influence last night. Mom was driving and got pulled over for the third time and arrested, meanwhile, Dad was arrested for drug possession? This can't be real life." He looks at his aunt and uncle. "I don't understand."

"I knew he started smoking again, but I didn't know about the other drugs he dabbled in." Uncle Tom clenches his fist. "I'm sorry, Killian. I wish I could have seen it."

"I'm just having a hard time wrapping my head around it." Killian rubs his face.

"We knew it was bad for your parents. I guess we didn't know to what extent." Aunt Ruth sits back in her chair. "We also found out your mom was fired from her job," she says gently.

"What happens now?" Ennis asks.

"We spoke with your parents through a social worker this morning." Uncle Tom produces a stack of papers. "And an adoption lawyer." He pauses to meet Killian's eyes to see if he should go on.

Killian sits up straighter. "Adoption lawyer?"

"We offered to become your legal guardians while your parents were handling their legal affairs and any rehabilitation they may need to go through."

"Then why would you need an adoption lawyer?"

"After speaking with the social worker and lawyers, your parents decided it would be in your best interest to live here with us permanently."

"Wait, Mom agreed with this?"

Uncle Killian and Aunt Ruth share a look that tells Killian it didn't go down that easily. Uncle Tom lets out a breath. "Not exactly. We had to wait for her to sober up first. Then she came to terms with her two options: you would either end up in the system or with us. Your dad got through to her that adoption would provide you with the stability that you need right now."

"OK, so that's it? My parents just give up?" Even though he doesn't want to go back with his parents, it still stings that they would so easily give him up. "They don't want me?"

Ennis leans into him, giving him the support he needs.

"Oh, Killi. No, sweetheart, this is far from easy for them. They love you so much. If you want to go see them, we can take you. They just didn't think you would want to see them in jail." Aunt Ruth's voice is a gentle balm.

"No, they were right. I don't want to see them like that." Killian shakes his head. "I'm sorry. I'm just . . . it's all happening so fast."

"Killi, what do you want?" Ennis asks what no one else has.

He holds her question for a moment, then lifts his head to look at his family. Meeting her eyes, he says, "I want you to adopt me. I really do."

Uncle Tom folds his hands in front of him. "There are a few steps in the adoption process, but we have started with your parents' consent. There will be a home study, and it has to be your choice, too. You will have to give a statement. In the meantime, we have been granted guardianship."

"So it will be official? I will really be part of this family?" Killian can't believe it; none of this feels like reality. The pain of his parents' choices, of losing them, mixes with the elation of having a family who chooses him.

"You have always been a part of this family, and your parents are, too, and they still are. What they have decided to do for you is incredibly selfless. I want you to see how much they love you to be able to see what their choices are doing to you and wanting you to be safe." Tom squeezes Killian's clasped hands, and Aunt Ruth places hers on top. Killian chokes up. Tears rain down his face. He doesn't have to return out into the storm; he gets to stay at his port, and he never has to leave it again.

"You are not rejected but protected, and we are choosing you. You may not be biologically ours, but you are very much a son to us," Ruth adds, reaching over to wipe the tears from his cheek. Her own tears join his.

Ennis places her hand on top of the pile of clasped hands. "Do you want this, Killian?"

Killian wants this, but with words lodged in his throat, he only nods his head.

"It's a lot to take in, Killi." Aunt Ruth's understanding gives him strength. "We have a counselor set up for you at the church to help you through all the emotions you will feel, and we don't need to change everything. You can still go to your school and do all the same things—" Killian stops his aunt.

"I want this, Aunt Ruth. I want to be here. I want this so much."

"Your mom and dad want you to know they love you. We will take you to see them whenever you are ready, and you may have phone calls if you want. They will still be a part of your life, as much as you want them to be," Uncle Tom reassures him.

Killian inhales through his nose; cinnamon and coffee—the scent of home—fills his lungs. He will never go a day without smelling that scent again. Ennis reaches over, wrapping her arms around him. Uncle Tom and Aunt Ruth get up to join them.

"I told you, Killi, paper or no paper, I will always choose you to be my brother."

Safe in the arms of his newfound family, he prays, thanking God for giving him not only his parents but this family. He may have a road to healing and forgiveness ahead, but like Mr. Daniels said, with God he will get through it. No matter what, he is chosen and he is loved.

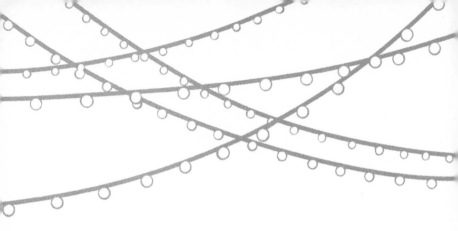

JESUS BE

AUDRAKATE GONZALEZ

With You at my side
And by faith, I might
Follow the path
To a future bright.
Not my way, but Yours—
Putting up the good fight,
A leader for others;
Jesus, be my light.

Open my eyes
To those all around—
The lonely and hurting,

Those who can't be found.
Giving voice to the silenced,
Let this be my mission.
I'll carry my cross;
Jesus, be my vision.

Give us compassion
To step into their story
Show them who You are;
You deserve all the glory.
We'll be sons and daughters,
Our striving will cease,
Brothers and sisters;
Jesus, be our peace.

Please, Jesus be.

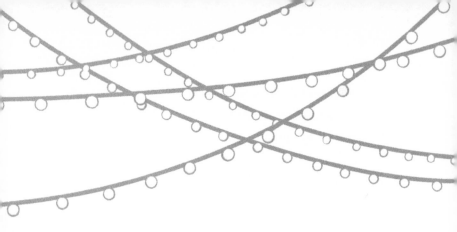

MASKS AND MASCARA

MORGAN J. MANNS

T he door closes behind me, and my steps lead me into the restroom. Lynn is hunched over a sink, her reflection in the mirror obscured by the rough brown paper towel she's using to wipe her face. I stiffen, feeling trapped.

My initial instinct is to run. But as my hand grips the door handle, I hesitate.

Looking back, I realize something unusual—she's alone. Where are her friends, the brutish girls that surround her like armor?

Every ounce of self-preservation urges me to leave. I'm not particularly eager to be ridiculed for my frizzy red hair, glasses, or my penchant for reading between classes. However, an unexplainable impulse holds me back.

I adjust my glasses and turn back toward Lynn. She doesn't appear as tough as usual. She's not lashing out at anyone. Instead, she almost reminds me a bit of the girl she once was—a little insecure but trying her best to hide it from the world.

I wasn't prepared for high school sharpening her edges into piercing daggers, and I certainly didn't think I'd be tossed away for a different crowd of friends. We were inseparable, once.

Lynn's gaze suddenly meets mine, her expression sour. "What do you want, *Kayla*?"

I wince at her snappish tone and start to turn around, forgetting about the past. Then I remember the silly promise we made to each other.

I turn back, surprised to hear myself speak. "Um, are you . . . okay?" The words sound forced to my ears, like my throat was scared to release them.

She averts her gaze, looking back at her reflection in the mirror. She's attempting to fix her makeup, but the streaks of black mascara tell a deeper story. She's not crying now, but her red-rimmed eyes suggest she has been.

Forcing myself to take a step forward, I remind myself that she wasn't always this unapproachable. I stand a little straighter, hoping my stature grants me courage.

"We used to be friends," I venture, my voice quivering

slightly. "We promised each other that no matter what happens, we would always be there for each other. You can tell me what's wrong."

She tears herself from the mirror and glares at me. I flinch but hold her gaze.

"That was when we were young and stupid," she scoffs. "We've both changed since we said those foolish words on the playground. It didn't help us then, and I doubt they'll help us now."

My heartbeat hammers in my ears. This conversation seems like it's going nowhere, but I feel like my old friend is somewhere under that mask of indifference and streaked mascara. She has to be there. I need to pull her out.

An old memory resurfaces, and I feel a kindling of hope. Perhaps it'll distract her into thinking of how things once were between us. "Remember when I fell off the monkey bars and that kid, Andy, laughed at me?"

She sniffs, and the corner of her mouth pulls into a grin. "Yeah, and I told him to knock it off or I'd never help him in math class again." Her eyes twinkle at the edges and I breathe a sigh of relief. I've found some of the old Lynn in there after all.

We break into giggles at the memory, sharing in the joy.

Lynn used to be a great friend, never hesitating to put her neck out for me. When did our friendship change? When did life get in the way and split us apart?

In less than a heartbeat, my smile dips into a disheartened frown. Lynn doesn't appear to see my change in expression, already looking back at the mirror, wiping away more of the mascara from her cheeks. With each dab of the paper towel, memories of the past flood into my mind. I swallow, suddenly remembering when I tried to help her through something far more difficult than playground bullies.

An apology forms in my mind as I come to realize what really drove us apart.

My chest compresses with the words I had stored up inside for all these years. They spill out in a torrent. "You always looked out for me, Lynn. I'm sorry I couldn't be there for you when you needed me the most. I don't blame you for finding different friends."

I had failed her at her weakest moment. Of course we drifted apart. I was the friend who couldn't figure out how to hold us together. Not her. She may have become one of the hardest girls in school, hiding behind layers of makeup and friends who would stand up for her in a fight, but I don't think that's who she really wanted to be. It's who she was forced to become—all because I couldn't be there for her.

Her small smile turns into a frown, mirroring my own, as she crumples the paper towel. She doesn't say I'm wrong. I know she's probably thinking of the same thing I am—of that defining moment in our path that set our friendship adrift.

I stand there, not sure what to say or do, waiting for her reaction. She looks like she's about to say something snappish, her face contorting into hard lines, her hands clenched into threatening fists. I tense, readying myself for the harsh words she has all the right to say to me. It looks like she's ready to snarl out another insult. But instead, she surprises me by turning away.

With a sigh, she grasps the counter with both hands and looks into the mirror, like maybe she, too, is trying to find the girl she once was. "It's . . . my dad," she finally says. A simple confession. "He's left again."

My heart sinks. That wretched man had left her family all those years ago in elementary school. It marked the beginning of the end of our friendship. Lynn's father's sudden abandonment devastated her, and I didn't know how to help. We were nine. How are we supposed to understand these kinds of things? Every book and fairy tale spoke of magical endings and happily ever afters. We weren't prepared for our lives crumbling down around us. I tried to build the pieces back up, sitting with her at recess as she cried under the play structure, offering her my favorite stickers, hoping it would somehow help. But it didn't. She was never the same. Neither was I. Our bond slowly faded, and now I realize that was the true turning point for us.

I heard a few months ago that he'd reentered her life. I was happy for her, hoping it was an answer to a burning prayer she'd had for so long. But now that he'd left again, she must be devastated. Tearing open an old wound only to pour salt into it was no way to treat a daughter. My eyes burn, feeling the heat of tears threatening to pour out of them.

"I'm sorry," I say, feeling heat rush into my cheeks. "If you want to talk about it, I'm here. It may not seem like it, but I always have been." I grasp my hands to keep them from trembling. Why can't I say something useful? Something that will actually comfort her. It feels like I'm falling back into the past, and there's nothing to catch me.

She remains silent, and I try to think of something else to say. I feel my own insecurities bubbling up, wishing I knew how to help better. This is playing out just like it did before, back when we were kids.

Her scowl softens. "I can't believe I'm saying this, but, yeah, sure. I could use someone to talk to. Just, don't offer me any stickers, okay?"

I walk closer, a small laugh escaping me. It's time to help an old friend. Only this time, I pray I can do it better than before.

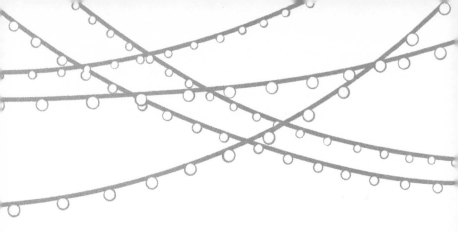

DEAR BOONE

ALI NOËL

Sometimes I watch you
and wonder
how such a little human
can feel things
so deeply
So hugely

I see you
sitting in the rain
And I long to scoop you up
shout, point
But look! The sparks!
There's happy magic here!

DEAR BOONE

It has taken me time to learn
that urgent cheers and
seeking shelter
isn't what every heart needs
Some can handle the rain
in all its dreary glory

When I watch you, my little boy
pitter-pattered by the water
I get scared you feel alone
and lonely
Blaming myself
for any sad complexities you carry

I have learned, more often than not
all you want
is for me to sit with you
And so, I do
Reminded once more
magic is here
because you are too

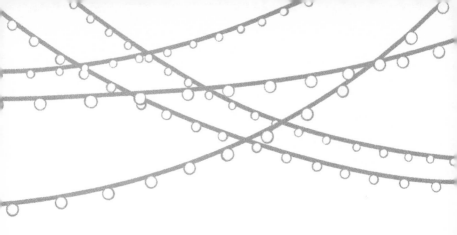

VIOLET

D.T. POWELL

"But, Dad, why does he have to stay with us?" Jared tipped his head toward the violet-skinned boy staring out their living room window. He looked about twelve, the same age as Jared. "He doesn't even speak our language."

Midmorning sun passed through the window's UV filter and made a bright puddle on the floor inches from Jared's black sneakers. With the toe of one shoe, Jared traced a line through the patch of sunlight. The deep green carpet flattened under his weight only to bounce right back into place moments after he'd touched it.

"His planet's been razed, son. There's nothing left except

a dead shell." Jared's dad held an extra comm disk. The little silver circle granted its owner access to the public info-net's extensive collection of books, vids, and news, as well as everything in its owner's private media collection. It kept track of everything around the house, too, even what was in the refrigerator.

"Why can't he stay with his relatives?" Another kid in the house would mean either Jared had to give up his room or he'd have to sleep ten feet away from a complete stranger. He didn't even know the boy's name. Dad had said it once, but it sounded so foreign that Jared couldn't recall it.

His dad tapped the thin, metal disk. A holographic menu hovered just above the device. His dad made two quick menu selections. "Rescue teams are still looking for his parents, and we don't know if he has other family. Jared, the world doesn't revolve around you." His dad's tone was firm but not unkind. "What if you were in his place? What if your mom and me were missing or dead, and everything you'd ever known was a smoldering heap? Remember last spring when you got lost in the mountains?"

Jared looked away, his stomach dropping as he recalled the fear of being alone with no one to help him. What would it have felt like to know his parents weren't coming to find him?

"Give him this." His dad handed him the disk and nudged him toward their guest.

The violet-skinned boy leaned toward the window. He watched a mockingbird dive out of the oak in the front yard, snag an insect, and return to a nest carefully woven into tree boughs.

Did they not have birds on his planet? Maybe they didn't. At least, not anymore. The news had talked about the intergalactic war, but Jared wasn't allowed to watch most of the video clips. The few he'd seen were faraway shots of destroyed cityscapes. He knew people used to live in those buildings, but he'd never considered what those vids truly meant.

Though dark circles ringed the boy's tired eyes and dirt smudged his face and hands, their guest looked just like any Earthborn kid—except for the deep purple skin. He smelled faintly of smoke and the musty odor of closely packed bodies.

How many transports had he taken to get here? He'd arrived a week later than the rest of the passengers in his group. In the confusion of getting out of his planetary system, had he missed a flight and had to sleep in a space terminal? How many days had he spent alone and afraid?

Jared's dad was right. He was being selfish.

He approached the boy and offered him the comm disk.

The boy took it, curious.

"Wanna go outside?" Jared said.

The boy almost dropped the disk in surprise.

"Sorry. Guess you don't have those where you're from." Jared shoved his hands in his pants pockets, fingers curling around the comm disk he always kept with him. He cleared his throat. "Well, how about it? You want to see some more birds?"

The boy stared at his new comm disk, then at Jared. "Yes." He nodded. "I would like to see the birds. It has been a long time since I saw them."

"Great! I'll show you my favorite bird-watching spot." Jared waved for the boy to follow him. "So . . . what's your name?"

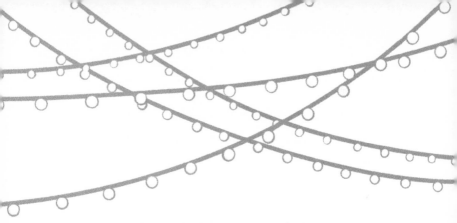

PRAYER FOR A FOSTER PARENT OF AN EMOTIONALLY CLOSED AND HURTING CHILD

YVONNE MCARTHUR

Lord, when all I see are empty spaces,
stone walls, tall turrets, and fastened gates,
bastions barred by anger and hurt,
a face carefully blank, as though
deaf to my words,
unmoved by gentle knocking,
indifferent—if not hostile—to the
warm touch of a palm on cold iron—
intervene.

God, I see a fortress, shut up tight,
its bright festival days a form of
misdirection,
the deep windows festooned to
distract from the pain inside.

But even the darkness is not dark to you, my Lord.

Immanuel.
God with us.
Jesus, who walks through walls,
sees the chained, oppressed, naked, and tormented,
and commands a legion of oppressors to come out
and be gone.
God who calls us each by name.
God who spoke into the void and said,
"Let there be light!"
This child may be beyond my reach,
but not beyond yours.

Go where I cannot.

Walk through fortress walls,
journey into dungeons of despair,
banish stabbing memories,
bind up lies,
unshackle truths,

speak tenderly,
coax this child into your arms,
and rub your soothing balm into
chafed wrists, battered hearts, bruised spirits,
and hope-lost souls.

God, who restored life to a widow's son,
called a daughter to rise from the dead,
and welcomed all children,
do so here and now, again.

I entrust to you
this child and the
seen and unseen griefs, injuries, and hurts
in this child's heart.

I entrust to you
my efforts, my hopes, and my sorrows.
I ask for strength—
please, Lord,
keep me faithful
in this loving work.

You are God Almighty and *kind.*

Amen.

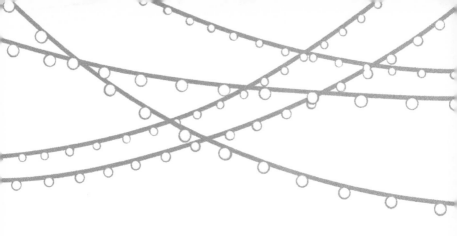

PHOENIX

DENICA MCCALL

Memory is a funny thing. It's often an imposter. But sometimes, it seems as if it's reaching from the deep folds of time to communicate something important. Something true.

The problem is, I don't know how to identify the difference between the lies and reality.

I adjust myself behind my sister on the flat, dusty ground, lifting the edge of my cloak over her small, five-year-old body and pulling her against me as I tuck the fabric under her shoulder. There's nothing but dry land surrounding us, with the occasional bush or tree to provide meager protection from the elements. Or nighttime predators. In the far distance, clumps of thorny brambles surround the wilderness. I remember people saying the thorns grew there because of a curse cast by another woman born with magic and eventually rejected by our village, but I know nothing more. The thorns haven't done anything except creak and moan. All the same, I shudder and bend my face to my sister's hair when their sound reaches my ears.

We've slept on the bare earth for so long now that dirt is permanently woven into our dark curls. It's pushed its way into our pores, but I've grown used to the feeling. I trust the elements more than the hearts of people.

A gust of wind rushes over us, making the fire dance wildly to one side. I shiver against Chyler's back. Tightly clutching the frayed fringes of the cloak, I move my fist and gently press it against her chest, feeling the steady, warm beat of her pulse as the memory surfaces again.

The image of his eyes has woken me nearly every night for twelve years, that fragment of a memory that I wish would just dissolve into nothing rather than puncturing my heavy chest with a confusing mixture of sadness and hope. Both sentiments bring only pain.

I picture my father staring at me through the thin gaps between the wooden slats separating my room from the rest of the cottage. With flickers of sorrow lining his brow, he blinks away the sheen that's gathered over his green eyes. And then, without a word, he turns away. All I see is his back, his worn coat. And all I hear are his boots against the wood floor until he disappears around the corner.

He's afraid of my magic, of the heat within my bones. This curse I was born with.

Chyler shifts, turning to press into me and moaning softly. I savor the feel of her breath on my neck. When that servant brought her to me, I was thrilled and devastated all at once—to learn I had a sister and to know that she had been rejected just like me.

Her existence gave me renewed purpose.

I peer beneath the cloak to see the mark on her wrist that mirrors mine and trace the outline of the flaming torch with my thumb. It isn't marred like my own, warped from consistent attempts to scratch it off. And if I have any say, it never will be.

My fingers against Chyler's skin wake her. As her eyes slowly flutter open, I sigh and pull my hand back. I didn't mean to disturb her sleep. In fact, I hope she never experiences insomnia like I do.

"I'm not tired anymore, Phoenix." She yawns and grins, then frees her arms from the cloak and twirls a strand of my hair around one of her little fingers.

"Yes, you are. Of course you are."

I tickle her neck until she giggles and releases my hair.

When I stop, she sits up. I sigh again and make myself sit up, too, lifting my arms and letting the cloak billow behind us in the wind before pulling it back around our bodies. Chyler nestles deep against my shoulder, the knee of her crossed leg pushing into my thigh, and we stare into the flames.

The village we came from lies in the distance, and I can barely make out the shapes of its buildings. I look at the large thorny bushes that linger at the distant edges of the land, always creaking in the night like ghosts bearing ill warnings.

For a fleeting second, I think I see the shape of a person standing in front of the thorns, but when I blink, the form is gone. It's not the first time I've seen specters among the distant shadows in the middle of the night, but I know my mind is playing cruel tricks on me.

"Phoenix." Chyler breaks the quiet, her childish lilt crooning my name. "I like the sky. It has the stars and the moon."

I look at her upturned face, realizing that she'd been gazing at the canopy stretching above us while my thoughts ran untethered through my head. "So do I."

I lean my head down to my sister's brow and add softly, "The stars punch holes in the dark, just like us. Like fire."

"But no one will ever know about our magic," she answers, her eyes flicking to me.

My chest tightens.

They gave me a name, my parents, after I was born and they saw the mark on my wrist, after they felt the heat radiating from my infant body and the slow, tingling burn running along their nerves when they held me. Deyanira. *Destroyer*. It's the name they sent me away with. They used leather gloves to handle me until I was old enough to be spoon-fed and burp myself. Supposedly, the fire magic within me would burn them with too much contact.

Once I could eat without much assistance, I was never touched. Not until they brought my sister out here when she was but one year, a servant wheeling her along in a rackety wagon with a little bit of food and some clothes for when she grew older. They hadn't kept her as long as they'd kept me. I was sent out here when I was five, Chyler's age now. They probably reasoned that I'd be able to care for her. It was best that way, for I wouldn't wish the remembrance of a quarantined existence on anyone.

I renamed myself when I was ten, recalling the story of the mythical bird that rose from the ashes. But they had never bothered to name my sister, so I gave her one. Chyler. *Beloved*.

Father never knew how much he taught me in those five years that I was still in their home. His voice would float into my lonely room as he read stories to my mother while my fingers waltzed with the dust in the beams of lantern light coming through the cracks between those boards.

"They do know about our magic," I say to Chyler, coming back to the present. "They're just afraid of it."

"But why? It isn't bad."

"I know," I whisper, kissing the side of her head. "They don't understand how lovely you are. How much light and warmth you could offer them. You were meant to bring so much goodness into this world, Chy."

"You too, Phoenix."

Tears spring to my eyes. It's hard to imagine anyone actually wanting me, anyone actually seeing me as lovely and valuable. What if I *did* burn them to a crisp?

The fire shrinks down, and the night is cold. I stand, unclasping my cloak and leaving it with Chyler while I walk over and crouch, holding my hands above the flickering orange embers. A gentle prickling sensation runs down my arms until it reaches my hands and my fingers. Though the burning sensation from the magic always makes my heart race, it doesn't hurt. It swallows me with a strange mix of comfort and excitement. When I touch it, the blackened wood reignites and the flames grow, higher and higher until they're licking my palms. Satisfied, I return to Chyler, my pulse gradually settling as I draw her into my lap and smooth her unruly hair until she's sound asleep.

Dawn wakes us both, though I don't remember dozing off.

We fill the following day with activities that we've become accustomed to, things we do to survive as well as not lose our sense of humanity. I teach Chyler how to sharpen a knife and how to hold it so that she won't cut herself. I hunt for our lunch and supper and begin carving a small bow for my sister, her very own that I'll soon teach her to use.

The wind hasn't ceased. In fact, it's grown stronger, driving against us and whistling through the branches of the scarce trees scattered about. The crisp air invigorates me. Chyler and I dance with our arms outstretched, letting the wind carry our raucous shouts wherever it wishes. I pick her up and spin her, our bursts of laughter disappearing into the bold currents. At dusk, I realize how much the wind has sapped my energy, so I sit hard in the dirt and allow myself to fall back, watching the sky turn from blue to orange to purple and finally gray while Chyler plays on her own. The sound of her feet scuffing the dry dirt brings a smile to my lips. She hums contentedly, and for a moment, all is well in our little world.

Chyler screams, and I shoot upright. I'm relieved to find her standing a few paces out, both hands covering her mouth.

A silhouette of a man approaches from the village, which I now notice is concealed by angled, shadowy shapes. The wind has been so loud today that I only now hear how the typical groaning of the thorn bushes at the perimeter of the clearing has grown into a roar. They sound like disjointed rhymes heralding imminent danger.

But I don't sense that the threat is directed at me or my sister. I gasp when it hits me. The thorns no longer surround the clearing—they've moved in upon the village.

I stand and run to Chyler, sweeping her into my arms and watching, warily, as the figure comes closer, his form emerging from the cluster of shadow where the village lies. He finally halts before us, and I can see him now in the moonlight, hands on his knees and sweat dripping down his temples. He forces himself upright and utters one word.

"Please—"

I've never seen him before. He's young, and a mass of dirty blond hair sweeps over his dark eyes.

"He sent me to fetch you," he says—urgent—though his eyes are clouded with uncertainty. "The thorns—" He casts his gaze to the perimeter where the thorny brambles once sat. "They've come to life and are attacking the village! Please, he said you could help."

The man's eyes shift to Chyler before returning to me. I squeeze her tighter.

I'm trembling, so unsure. He? Who is *he*? And why would I help the people who have done nothing but reject me? They only came to us as a last resort. How could I . . . But the man's eyes, they pierce me with desperation. Not only that, but he's so *real*. I haven't interacted with another human for so many years that his presence tugs at me and sends a swirl of confusing emotions through my belly. If the thorns are attacking the village, I can't very well let everyone die. Can I?

"Let's go," Chyler whispers in my ear.

I nod once to the man and follow him as he turns and walks briskly back toward the village. I can't have my little sister thinking I've lied to her about what she could offer the people if they only gave her a chance. As conflicted as I feel, perhaps this is her chance.

When we come upon the village, the brambles are closing in on every side, moving like large, crooked skeletons. Like monsters intent on consuming their prey. I see a large one snatch a man by the collar of his shirt. It lifts him into the air before its thorny limbs pierce his body in far too many places. The thorny creature drops the limp man to the ground. I stare, horrified, the screams of the villagers consuming my head as the man's body lies lifeless and bloody on the ground. Everyone is running, fighting back, or being picked up and pierced by these ruthless monsters. There's blood everywhere. The village will be destroyed. I look to Chyler. Her small brow is drawn at the sight, but determination sparks in her eyes. I want to shield her, but I can't extinguish the fire I see within her. My little sister has come alive, even in the midst of death.

The young man turns and calls to me. "Set them ablaze. Destroy them!" He thrusts his hand toward the bony monsters that creak and snap with each small, deadly movement.

Deyanira. Destroy.

But I don't want to be a destroyer. I want to be accepted, valued for my existence and not only what I can offer. I want to make souls burn with the same passion I feel. I want to know what the fire in my blood is destined to awaken. To bring *life*.

But I won't have that chance if I let death have its way.

Chyler wriggles out of my arms. She's running, running fearlessly toward the thorny beasts, past the messenger. Before I can cry out, her hand encircles one of the crooked branches. It ignites. She takes hold of another, and the same thing happens. She whirls and pins me with an innocent gaze as her hair hits her face.

"We have to save them!" she shouts.

It's her courage that sparks the blaze in me.

So I join her, grabbing the branches one by one, heedless to the thorns that cut my palms, the blood that streams down my arms. We set the monsters on fire so that soon, the whole mass of them is burning, tumbling, caving in on itself. I sweep my arms, willing my magic to command the flames and the thorns they consume to move away from the village, to keep the houses, buildings, and people from burning too. Chyler follows my lead. Our efforts are successful. Surprised, I feel heat and energy rushing through my arms in waves—stronger than it's ever been. I didn't realize we could actually control an object on fire without touching it.

As we back away, we watch the brambles burn. My body smashes into the young man who fetched us, and he catches my shoulders. He dips his head when I turn to regard him. He has kind eyes. But more than that, he *touched* me.

And he's still touching me.

The man sucks in a breath as if only now realizing that the contact is causing him pain. But he doesn't let go, even when I turn to face him completely. He holds my shoulders steady and claims my gaze, the light from the blaze behind us flickering over his features.

"Incredible," he says. "It only hurts with initial contact. But then . . ." He pauses, eyes wide. "I feel . . . more alive than ever. Like I could do anything." A small laugh escapes his lips.

I cave under the honesty of his words. He didn't praise me for destroying the thorns. Instead, he marveled at the life within my veins. Not only that, but I'm not burning him. I stand there, unsure what to say, only faintly aware that my young sister is sprinting back toward the flames. I turn, then, to see what she could possibly be doing, and am astonished to find her with her arms stretched to either side. She finishes what we started, her magic causing an unseen force that pushes the burning monsters apart, making a safe, yawning path to the village.

The young man nudges me. "Your father," he breathes. "He's the one who sent me."

Not knowing what to say to that, I turn away from him and go stand by my sister. Chyler is staring at the village, at the people bleeding on the ground. Placing a hand on the side of her head, I press her face gently against my hip, shielding her from the bloody mess. Some of the villagers who are still alive look at us, a mix of fear, wonder, gratefulness, and shame displayed on their faces. A man makes his way through the carnage, his gaze intent on me.

When he reaches us, he strokes Chyler's hair as tears begin to roll down his blood-smeared cheeks. Then his green eyes find mine.

I can't breathe. I know my face is streaked with tears as well. Dirty. Sweaty. When he puts a hand on my cheek, I suck in a breath at the pain that ignites as my conflicted thoughts collide with his gentleness.

I can't remember feeling his touch, ever.

It's possible he's never felt mine.

"I never wished to send you away," Father says, his voice low and soothing, a voice I remember. "The village elders insisted on it. Said they'd kill you if we even tried to visit." His voice cracks and his chest shudders as I try to take it all in. "But there were times I would come in the dead of night, just to see if you were okay. It was a risk, but I had to—" His words break on a sob. "—I had to see you. I'm so sorry I couldn't do more. They had ways of finding out."

I let out a small gasp, thinking of the specter standing at the edge of the clearing, haunting me on those nights I couldn't sleep. "That . . . was you?"

Father nods. "Oh, I so longed to come to you both. To hold you."

"But you locked me up in that room. You were afraid," I whisper, searching his face.

The thorns surrounding the village have become embers. I can smell smoke, but the flames have shrunk. Behind us, healers are tending to the injured. People whimper. Some walk around aimlessly, as if unsure how to keep on after such a tragedy, while others watch us with interest.

"Yes, I was afraid back then," Father admits. "Your mother fell ill after your birth, and I mistakenly set the blame on you. I thought your magic somehow caused her illness, and I didn't want it to worsen. But I was wrong, Phoenix. I was so wrong, and it didn't even make logical sense. Every day of my life I've regretted keeping you in that room and having to send you away."

My brow draws together. "Phoenix?"

"Yes."

"But . . . you called me Deyanira."

Now it's his turn to wear a furrowed brow. "No, I never called you that. The enforcers must have told you that was your name when they sent you away."

"What?" I whisper, trying to recall such a thing. I look back up at him. "What about Chyler?" I ask, gesturing to my sister at my side. Her eyelids are heavy but she wears a small, tired smile.

"Your mother passed away after giving birth to her," my father says. "The elders allowed me to keep her and hire a nurse to care for her until she was a year old, but then I was forced to send her away, too."

Chyler reaches her hand out to take his. "It's all right," she whispers.

It's too much. I collapse against my father's strong frame, overcome by sobs that weaken my body. How can it be? Have I truly believed a lie for this long?

"You are my daughter, Phoenix. And I will cherish you forever. Both of you," Father is saying. "Not just because of your magic that I know can restore life and warmth to this hurting village. But because you belong to me."

In my mind's eye, I see his eyes—his eyes from before— how they'd gloss over until he'd blink the moisture away. I hear his voice, reading stories from the next room.

Reading stories to *me*.

And as I sink against him, my memories dissolve into ashes along with the brambles we set alight until they rise into something new.

Memory is a funny thing that way.

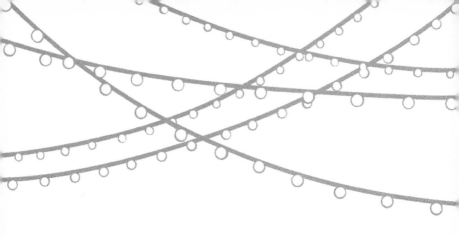

ECHOES OF CHILDHOOD

NATHANIEL LUSCOMBE

The echoes of childhood
have long since faded
from the eyes of those
who grew up too fast.

Their innocence stolen,
the weight of adulthood
laid upon young shoulders.
Their souls seek hope.

I see the footage on the news;
their headlines shock me—

these stories should only be found
in the pages of history.

Have we moved forward
and left the children behind?
Have we traded their joy for our comfort
and left them to pay the price?

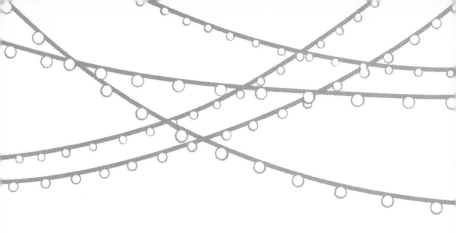

JEMMA'S
SPECIAL FRIEND

JADE LA GRANGE

She's here!" Jemma's mom called from the living room.

Abandoning her plastic ponies, five-year-old Jemma ran from her bedroom. She skidded across the kitchen floor and landed right before the front door. All Jemma had been told was that this stranger was to be a part of their family for a while. She clapped her hands and bounced up and down, ready to greet the mysterious guest.

The doorbell chimed. Jemma slowly turned the doorknob.

Jemma dragged out opening the door, wondering if the person behind it was going to be a magical nanny with a bottomless bag of fun or a whimsical walking cane or—

"Hello, Jemma. I'm Bernadette, your family's new au pair. I've heard plenty about you."

As swift as lightning, shyness struck Jemma at the sight of a girl much older than her. She had long brown hair tied back in a ponytail. She wore just a plain T-shirt, jeans, and sneakers.

Jemma stared at Bernadette, eyes wide.

"Jemma, aren't you going to welcome our guest inside? You know Momma can't get up easily to do so," Jemma's mom said with a raspy softness, a deafening cough following right after.

Jemma let out a little sigh. Her momma was sick with an illness that kept her from moving around the house very much. She had been sick for a long time, but it got worse when Daddy left. Since then, Momma struggled with completing even the smallest of tasks at home. Cooking spaghetti Bolognese, Jemma's favorite meal, was like wrestling with a pot of snakes for Momma. And whenever Momma gave Jemma a piggyback ride, she'd tease Jemma that she felt as heavy as an elephant on her back. But Jemma knew that couldn't be quite right because she was definitely smaller than an elephant.

It all made sense to Jemma one day when, smiling through tears, Momma said that she couldn't carry on playing like that anymore with her.

It wasn't this hard for Momma when Daddy was still around. He was able to do all the things that Momma no longer could do, and he didn't writhe in pain when he played with Jemma. Things became so much harder when he ran away. Jemma wished he'd just come back home. But the way Momma cried the night he left meant that Daddy was going to be away for longer than forever.

But even so, Bernadette was not going to replace Daddy. Not if Jemma had something to say about it first.

"Daddy ran away to join the circus." At least, that's where Jemma thought he went. "Try and beat that."

Bernadette knelt and looked straight into Jemma's eyes.

Jemma wanted to back away, but something about Bernadette's soft smile kept her still.

"You're right. I can't do that." Bernadette murmured, "All that I'm here to do is bring a smile to your face every day and make your mom feel no pain as your family's new au pair."

"What is an au pair?" Jemma asked, courage growing.

Bernadette smiled, placing a hand tentatively on Jemma's shoulder. "As your family's au pair, I'm here to help you and your momma, especially when things get really, really hard. If there are bad times and storms, I will be sure to protect you any way I can." Then, as if on cue, thunder boomed in the clouds above.

Jemma shrieked, eyeing Bernadette with curiosity. Was Bernadette actually . . . magic?

Before Jemma could wonder more about the possibility, Bernadette stood up. "First order of business is to get a tour of your house. Starting with the best room: your bedroom," Bernadette proclaimed.

Jemma's smile curved like an upside-down rainbow. "Yes,

yes! It's this way! It's pink with butterfly stickers and star-shaped fairy lights . . ." Jemma rambled on and on as she let Bernadette walk into her home, closing the door behind her.

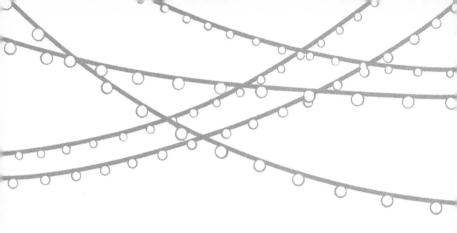

IT'S NOT
A CHILD'S PLACE

SARAH ANNE ELLIOTT

It's not a child's place to ask to be loved,
To call for a kiss or request a hug.
But when standing at the door, all she could think
Was how utterly afraid she was, and her heart started to sink.
Little girls don't ask to be loved; they just wonder why
Adults get busy, and they never look
No matter how hard you try.
So little girls call and they keen,
They cry and wonder what it could mean,

Because how hard is it, they ask,
To love me behind this big empty mask?
They ask for presents, toys, and dolls—
For surely love could be bought at the mall.
When she is grown up, lonely and old,
Even if she did everything she was told,
She'd be alone and judged—
For it isn't a child's place to ask to be loved.

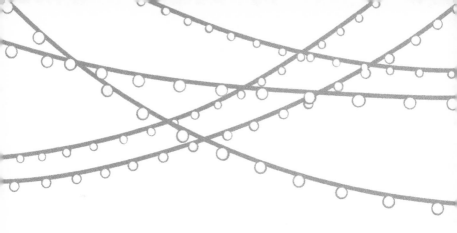

PINK CLOUDS

SHANA BURCHARD

I remember the pink clouds with my mother. The way they outlined the fading purple sun and melted into the horizon. I sat watching them in the land of warmth and wars. The place where I came from. The place where my mother died.

"Red sky at night, sailor's delight," she used to tell me with a wink. It was an English phrase she learned from the missionaries who visited us each week in our *nyumbani*. I remember looking up at her curling black hair as she would hum me a sweet song to sleep.

Chosen and beloved, my baby is to me. Sweet child of mine, love eternal. To see your face is to see God's blessing.

She was a reader and would read the books the missionaries gave her. She would tell me stories of faraway lands and the hope they gave. "But do not hope in the land, *mwanangu*. Hope for things unseen. Hope in the God of pink clouds who created them." And I would watch as she set determined dark eyes on the skyline. But she was not watching the clouds. She was looking for Someone beyond them.

At times, she would gently chide me for focusing on myself. "*Mwanangu*, you must refocus on God. Remember the missionaries' teachings. This selfishness must end." She would gently pat my hand in the old tradition. "*Mwanangu*, this selfishness does not become you. You were created to be a child of the King. Put your hope in Him. Do not place yourself on the throne. There is a true and living hope beyond this little village." She would take me outside to look for pink clouds made by the Creator.

I looked for pink clouds while I watched the skies and hoped for something unseen. I did this while I watched the skies turn to fire and ash. As I watched it burn anger and hatred on my village. I watched it as it rained gray clouds of sorrow as I read the symbol over my mother, the two beautiful ovals joined to mean "forever" with a diamond in the middle. *Nyame biribi wo soro.* God is in the heavens. The God of hope the missionaries told me of.

After some time, the missionaries brought me here, in the land of the eagle. And I followed in the footsteps of my mother. I read and studied the clouds. This land of freedom tasted sweet, but selfishness ran deep in its soil. At every turn, a promise of freedom was etched into its ground. But counterfeit freedom in the land of the eagle was nothing like the freedom I had been given.

Yes, I was grateful for my life here and for the missionaries' provisions. But my hope lay in things eternal, not in the works of my own hands. Whether across the sea or here in this land, my soul was content.

When I had my daughter, I named her after my mother. *Oluchi.* Work of God. I would sing her my mother's tune in my native tongue.

Chosen and beloved, my baby is to me. Sweet child of mine, love eternal. To see your face is to see God's blessing.

I would smile upon her face and look up at the sky, searching for pink clouds beyond the hills like white elephants.

I looked for the Creator of the clouds when all I could see was creation. I settled my heart in a hope beyond the present. And I am thankful for a life of pink clouds when others cannot see beyond hills. I am thankful for things unseen.

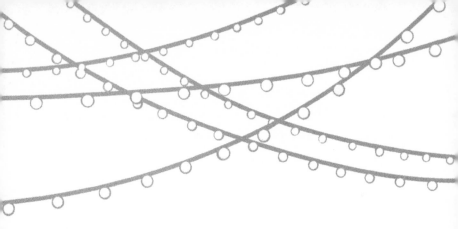

BOOK OF FLOWERS

ANNE J. HILL

She picks flowers at every stop
On this broken life of hers
Presses them in a weatherworn book

The bleeding heart was from
Her father's garden where
She used to hide away
When the yelling burst her ears

The black-eyed Susan she took
From the curb outside the hospital
She slept in the waiting room

While her mother faded away—
A blanket placed over her shoulders
By a nurse at the end of her shift

The daisy is from the lady
Who found her living on the streets
And brought her to her RV
To share a bowl of soup

The rose she stole from the family
Who couldn't be bothered to
Pick her up from school

The baby's breath is from the
Group home where she caught
Bronchitis but told no one at all

The dandelion she picked
While camping under the stars
Alone in a wild meadow
That turned out to belong
To a man with a rifle

The red amaryllis she plucked
From the lady with a garden
Spilling through her house
Who always sang her to sleep

The iris was given to her
By a child that she met
While huddled on the streets

The poinsettia was from the postman
Who let her crash on his couch
On her twentieth birthday

And today, she picks a daffodil
From the little garden she planted
With her two baby girls
At the house she now calls home

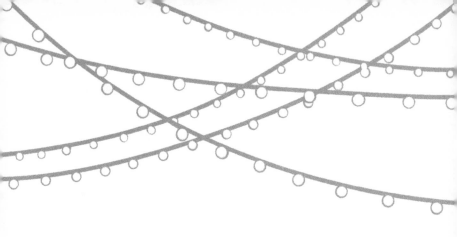

THE BLACKTIDE

MORGAN J. MANNS

Belany clutched her spear against her silver-scaled torso, propelling herself through the murky water with powerful kicks of her tail. She glanced over her shoulder. Among the dense kelp reeds, a dozen glowing eyes tracked her through the darkness. Pushing down her fear, she surged deeper into the ocean's depths.

She had stolen something precious, and now she was paying the price. But if she crossed back into her home territory, the creatures following her wouldn't dare pursue her. She kicked with furious strides. Home wasn't much farther. She would be safe there.

As a skilled warrior, Belany understood her limits. She

wasn't fully grown, and her scaled armor hadn't completely hardened past her chest. As she was, confronting a swarm of Swarfali tracker eels was impossible. Even facing one would be a challenge.

She swam desperately, her gills flaring. If she crossed the border between their tribes, patrolling warriors would scare off these creatures. She just had to ensure the patrols didn't see her either. If they did, they'd question why she was in enemy territory, and she didn't have an answer that would satisfy them.

Hearing the snapping jaws from the eels behind her skipped her heart into an even faster rhythm. Her eyes darted for somewhere to hide—a cowardly move, but she preferred not to die. She knew what kind of monster would be controlling those eels.

For a moment, she considered abandoning the small sack secured at her waist, leaving it for the creatures. The small Krystal seeds within were what the Swarfali eels wanted, after all. The precious items she had stolen from their masters.

She immediately withdrew the thought. She would not give up so easily.

In a swift move, she plunged into a deep trench, aiming to lose the pursuers with the sudden change in route. It was a risk —the eel's keen eyes worked better than hers in the darker ocean waters. She'd be at a disadvantage if they caught up to her.

Her gaze fell on a promising cluster of openings along the

trench. Her tail twitched. She could lose the creatures in that labyrinth of tunnels.

Just before she entered the largest opening, a slim, webbed hand emerged from a rocky crevice to her left.

Belany spun, her spear poised at the figure behind the jagged rocks. Her face contorted into a snarl as she braced herself for another fight.

Her spear halted just inches from her wide-eyed little sister, who defensively raised her hands.

"Yena, what are you *doing*?" Belany lowered her spear and grabbed her sister, pulling her into one of the caves. She tried not to think about how close she had been to driving the tip through her sister's unprotected neck.

Yena fidgeted nervously. "I . . . I followed you. You shouldn't be out here."

Belany didn't know how her sister had remained hidden from her sight for so long, but she supposed Yena always did have a way of blending in with her surroundings. The subtle, dappled hues of her green scales gave her sister perfect camouflage.

"You shouldn't be here either!" Belany scolded in hushed tones. "It's dangerous. Your tail scales haven't even hardened yet—if the Swarfali happen to see you, they won't give a second thought to killing you!" Her eyes flicked to the entrance, hoping she'd finally rid herself of the swarm of eels.

Yena's angular face fell into a scolding frown. "You went to find the Krystals." It wasn't a question. "And now the

Swarfali are chasing *you* as you flee their waters. Why did you do it?"

Belany's stern expression softened and she refrained from looking at the sack secured at her waist. "Someone had to try."

Two years had passed since the most recent Blacktide calamity, an inevitable natural plague that circled the ocean, cast its shadow upon their tribe. Their once pristine waters fell into an inky abyss. Initially, hope lingered among their people. The waters had ebbed in their murkiness before—past calamities swept away by the tides in due time. The elders preached patience, urging everyone to wait for the waters to clear, but for Belany's family, waiting was no longer an option. Two years was longer than any other Blacktide calamity, and with their mother's swelling belly, they were running out of time. They needed the Krystals now, despite the small seeds being banned by the elders. Any day, their baby brother would be born, and his new gills wouldn't survive the murky waters without them.

Yena swam toward Belany, resting a hand on her shoulder. "You shouldn't have to take on this burden alone. You can ask for help, you know." Her sister spoke with more maturity than any other fourteen-year-old Belany had ever met. It was difficult for her to remember that she was the older sister sometimes—four years separated them.

Belany sighed, her tail flicking with unease. The Blacktides created an unexpected division among their people. While their elders trusted that the waters would eventually clear on their own, others—like Belany—sought protection against the effects of the silted waters, even though doing so was edging on treason.

The small Krystals were originally brought from a distant part of the ocean by nomadic merfolk years ago, who insisted they protected the youngest's lungs from the worst of the dark waters. Many within Belany's tribe were intrigued by the tiny translucent seeds streaked with sunshine-yellow veins, but the elders refused to accept the foreign medicinal knowledge, turning the nomads and their Krystal seeds away. As the elders reminded everyone, the Way of the Spear, their creed, was to survive based on what grew around them naturally. They would not plant these unknown entities in their waters, and they would not use them on their youngest. If the babies survived the Blacktide on their own, the elders promised the Way of the Spear would honor their battle by strengthening them into mighty warriors.

Belany believed in the Way of the Spear, but she also knew their people were dying. Quickly. And if she had to watch her baby brother suffocate as he tried to flare his gills for the first time, she would never forgive herself. She had to try to save him, but she couldn't ask her sister for help. She purposely hadn't told Yena what she was doing to keep her sister safe. If the elders found out about this, her and her sister may never be allowed to return to their tribe. They'd be banished, forced to face the ocean on their own.

"I know this is foolish," Belany said, bringing her gaze

back to Yena. "But we can't just wait around for something that may or may not happen. The waters may never clear and then . . ." She didn't want to say it, the thought unbearable. Their brother would surely die.

The youngest among their kingdom were suffering, their lives slipping away as they struggled to draw breath amidst these murky Blacktides. Too many had already died. Belany shivered. Far too many. Every baby born in these conditions had only lasted a matter of days before the Blacktides claimed them. Their small gills couldn't filter the murky waters. Not one had survived to become the mighty warriors their elders claimed they could become.

When Belany heard the rumors that the rival Swarfali tribe across the trench had accepted the gift from the nomadic merfolk, successfully using the seeds to strengthen the children's immunity against the Blacktides, she knew she had to find out if it was true. If they had the Krystals, she could save her brother.

"Well?" Yena's eyes turned from accusing to hopeful. "Did you find them—the Krystals?"

"Do you really want to be involved with this?" Belany asked, already fearing the answer. If her sister chose this path, it could lead to a fate perhaps worse than death—banishment from their tribe.

Her sister's face twisted into hard lines. "Our brother needs us."

Belany nervously reached into the small sack secured at

her side, her fingers brushing against dozens of smooth seeds gathered hastily from the Swarfali gardens. She took one and unveiled it to Yena. No larger than a pearl, it rested in her palm —transparent and pure, like their waters once were.

"They're real." Yena said, reaching a tentative hand toward it.

With a nod, Belany carefully withdrew the small seed and stowed it in her pack—she knew how fragile they were, accidentally crushing the first one she picked from the odd silver-green plants growing out of the ocean floor. The internal substance, a thick paste, was meant for the children to ingest, helping strengthen undeveloped gills. She needed to get the Krystals home as quickly as possible. If she could prove their effectiveness, perhaps the elders would allow her to distribute them to the other newborns.

"Yena, we need to get these back to the tribe. When our baby brother is born, he may have a chance at life. We—"

Faint lights dotted the cave entrance. Sleek Swarfali eels took up positions, sealing them inside.

Belany brought a hand up over her mouth to signal Yena to be quiet. The two sisters drifted to the back of the cave, hidden in the shadows.

One of the largest eels drifted forward, snaking its head back and forth as if trying to catch their scent.

Yena suddenly gripped Belany's arm, causing her to swish her tail into the rock wall behind her. The metal clang snapped the eel's attention toward them.

They'd been spotted.

Belany brandished her spear, terror racing down her spine. "Stay behind me, Yena!"

The creatures inched closer, resembling sea snakes poised to strike. If only they were sea snakes. She could kill those easily enough.

Yena trembled, sending ripples through the water. Belany had to get her sister out of here. Her brow furrowed as she focused on the girl's strengths. She was young, yes, but there were advantages to her scales not being fully hardened. Her sister would be faster than her.

A plan formed and she hoped her sister would go along with it.

With slow, careful movements, Belany released one hand from her spear and began to untie the sack of Krystals from her waist.

"Belany, please, don't," Yena whispered urgently. "We need them."

Ignoring her sister, she held out the sack toward the eels. "Take these," she said. "I know your masters want them back."

The creatures stopped, regarding the sack with curious golden eyes.

As the largest one squirmed closer, its mouth agape as if wanting Belany to place the sack inside, Belany spun with a powerful kick of her tail. She pressed the pack into her sister's hand. "Go! Don't look back." In the same breath, Belany thrust her spear backward, impaling the eel. It released a torrent of erratic electricity, sending painful shocks down her arms. She bit back a scream at the same time she unintentionally released her spear. She had known the eel's electric attack would be painful, but this was a hundred times worse than she expected.

She flexed her fingers, attempting to coax sensation back into her numbed limbs. "Yena, hurry, take those to the newborns," she managed to utter through gritted teeth.

With a tight-lipped nod, Yena began swimming to the edges of the cave toward the entrance.

A series of ear-splitting screeches erupted from the swarm. She winced, knowing what was next—their instinct to attack a weakened prey was predictable. In a second, they'd surround her, forgetting about Yena. Then her sister could escape and—

The swarm screeched again and disappeared back the way they came, leaving a wake of bubbles.

Belany blinked slowly, meeting her sister's confused gaze.

Why would they have left so suddenly?

Movement from the dying eel turned her attention. Its internal light flickered from yellow to black as it struggled against the spear still impaled in its side. It drifted to the cave floor, its movements becoming increasingly feeble.

Yena swam back in front of Belany, taking her hands. "We need to go *now*, before they come back."

A feeling of vulnerability crept up Belany's scales. She couldn't retrieve her spear until the eel was dead—the defensive electricity would still be coursing through it. If the swarm came back, they'd be defenseless.

Her eyelids felt heavy, and she worked to keep them open. She was suddenly too tired to even think about wielding a spear. The shock had taken its toll on her limbs, making her weary. With a long glance at the still struggling eel, she let her sister lead her toward the entrance.

Then, another darker shadow moved across their exit. The eel's master had arrived.

Belany halted, tightening her grip around her sister's hand.

A large figure glided fully into view, taking up the entire entrance—a Swarfali warrior. "You have something of ours," he said, his voice booming.

The eel's flickering light illuminated the merman's muscular frame, a dark contrast to Belany and Yena's graceful silhouettes. As a full-grown male, his body was completely covered with impenetrable scaled armor, from the curve of his black and silver tail to the base of his neck. His face all sharp angles and contempt. Clenched firmly in his grip was a trident, a symbol of his elevated rank in the Swarfali army. It was pointed firmly at them.

Belany's heart hammered against her chest. With scales like that, she knew they had dispatched one of their finest warriors to pursue her.

Beside her, Yena straightened herself to her full height, flaring her tail beneath her. "Let us leave, traitor! You have no right to keep us here."

Belany winced at her sister's boldness. She was right to call him a traitor—his people were separatists from their tribe, no longer following the Way of the Spear, but provoking him was no way to try and survive this skirmish.

Looking at him, it was hard to fathom that they were once all the same tribe, centuries ago. Across the trench, the Swarfali merfolk had adapted to their waters by adopting a black sheen to their scales to blend into the Blacktide. In Belany and Yena's tribe, they still shifted between bright blue scales and soft green, a testament on how the waters should look.

Looks weren't the only difference between their two tribes. Centuries ago, his ancestors believed there was strength in accepting outside aid when needed. When the elders disagreed, a number of merfolk left to forge the Swarfali tribe across the trench, causing strife and anger between the two tribes. A treaty had been formed to ensure everyone stayed in their own area of the ocean. If anyone should cross, they were to be killed.

The merman scoffed, jerking his chin in Belany's direction. "*She* violated the treaty by crossing the trench into our waters. I'm only here to reclaim what rightfully belongs to the Swarfali." He opened his hand expectantly toward them. "Return the Krystals, and I might overlook you calling *me* a traitor."

They were trapped. Belany knew they couldn't outrun or attempt to fight a full-grown warrior. She clenched her teeth, hating that she'd come so close to helping her brother live, only to die before she could even meet him.

Knowing she had little choice, she extended her hand toward him with the sack of Krystals. Maybe if she gave them back, he'd let them go. She couldn't risk her sister's life, even if it meant dooming her unborn brother's.

"Swarfali will always be traitors," Yena said. "Your people left ours, making your own tribe. If you're not a traitor, you're at least a descendant of one. Take your Krystals and let us go."

The male regarded them with fierce eyes, accepting the sack. He cradled them more gently than Belany could have imagined. His voice sharp, he growled out, "*Your* people don't believe in using anything to help against the Blacktide. It's why my ancestors left in the first place. What are you even doing out here, risking your lives for Krystals? Perhaps if I'm a traitor, you are one as well." He made no move to let them pass.

Belany growled low at the accusation, which only elicited a chuckle from the Swarfali. Yes, she had stolen from the Swarfali, hoping to use banned medicinal knowledge on her family, but she still felt like she belonged in her tribe.

Her temper rising, she said, "I am no traitor. I just want my baby brother to live!" Unexpected heat rose to her face and she clenched her hands into fists.

His sly expression fell into a softer one. "Too many lives have been lost to the Blacktide. When will your elders recognize that change needs to happen?" He sighed, his eyes closing long enough for Belany to warrant a look down at the eel. Electricity still flared off of it. She wouldn't be able to retrieve the spear in time to attack, and even if she tried, her limbs were still aching with fatigue.

He opened his eyes again. "Traditions are important, but having the ability to recognize when to accept help from others is a strength of its own."

Belany regarded his words, her clenched fists slowly relaxing. He was . . . right. It was time for the elders to accept the inevitability of change. The ocean itself was a place where creatures needed each other for survival. The shark was mighty but could never survive without the small fish that cleaned the sticky Blacktide plankton from its body. If the mighty shark didn't turn away help, why should the merfolk have to?

After a moment of uncomfortable silence, the Swarfali male began to turn back toward the entrance.

Belany's tail twitched and she tensed again. Was he calling back his eels to kill them? She tried to force Yena behind her, but the male turned and she froze.

"I'll tell you what," he said, tossing the sack gently through the water toward the girls. Belany caught it. "Take these precious Krystals to your brother and the rest of the families who need them. Show the elders and your people they work. If they won't accept it, come and join us. We will protect you."

Belany gasped. He was letting her have them? Just like that?

"Just remember this," he continued as he eyed his trident,

"maybe there's no need to fight between our people anymore. Perhaps if your elders are willing, we can teach you to grow Krystals, and together we can work to combat the Blacktides and survive. Treaties can be changed."

As he left, leaving the two girls in the cave alone to mull over his words, Belany couldn't help but feel a swell of hope. She looked at the sack of Krystals in her hands. Maybe this was the beginning of a better future for all of the merfolk.

With a look of shared understanding between the two sisters, they left the cave, heading back to their home to rescue their brother and the rest of the children who needed them. Belany had a feeling this wasn't the last time she would see the Swarfali. If the elders persisted in their reluctance to heed reason, she might need to seek him out once more. She would save her family, one way or another. Her brother's life depended on it.

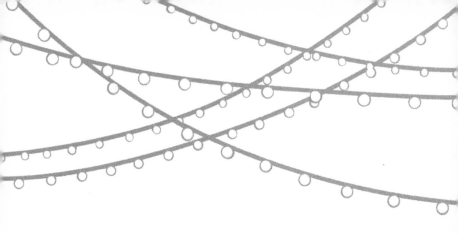

FOR YOU I PRAYED

BROOKE J. KATZ

For you I prayed,
Our little one.

In my womb, I did not carry,
But in my heart you've always been.

God hand selected you,
Entwining our lives for eternity.

Heart to heart, we are connected;
Such a gift you are.

Our little one,
For you I prayed.

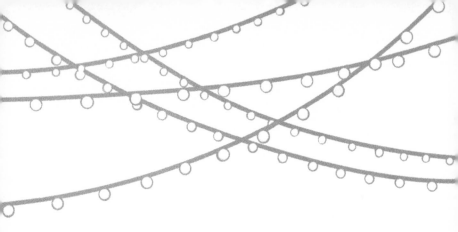

A BOOK FOR SOPHIE

D.T. POWELL

Lane Harris sat on his couch, waiting for seven-year-old Sophie to put her shoes on so they could leave for the park. Her grandparents were out of town until Friday, and she'd already asked to go to the park five times in the past day and a half, but the rain hadn't stopped until this morning.

He slipped his keys from the pocket of his jeans. Just two years ago, he'd been jobless and living in Sophie's grandparents' guest room. Now, he had a house, a decent used car, and regular work. But the day he'd been handed the deed to his friend's home was bittersweet. What was a house compared to a person?

He tucked the keys away and crossed the living room. Atop the fireplace's mantle stood a battered paperback, flanked by a picture and a funeral program dated mere months before he'd moved into this house—Sophie's former home.

The name printed on the program cover was in bold, elegant letters. Victoria Leigh Garrison. Below her name sat the date of her birth and the day she died. Thirty-five short years. It was one thing to lose someone twice his age, but Vic had been only a few months younger than him when death took her.

Opposite the program, Vic's photo smiled at him. Somehow, this image had captured the light in her eyes—coffee brown, just like Sophie's. He didn't usually care for photos. Too many memories of his old life and all the mistakes that went with it. But this picture held so much more than reminders of past failings. Even as cancer slowly stole her life, this woman had been a friend to him. He'd lost everyone and everything, but Vic had stood by him. He was alive because of her. How he wished she could be here to see her little girl growing up.

"Mommy loved going to the park." Sophie pulled on her blue jacket. She looped the laces on one pink and white sneaker, then the other, and dashed to Lane, ready to leave.

He smiled at her persistent energy. "I met your mom at the park once."

"I remember." Sophie stood on tiptoe in front of the fireplace. The top of her head missed the mantle by several inches, and even craning her neck did little to add to her height. "That's when Mommy gave you her book." She pointed to the worn volume.

Lane picked up the thick fantasy novel, holding it with care. He didn't want to fray the already bent edges of the cover or add another crack to the dilapidated spine. A ruggedly dressed man holding a short sword filled half the cover. His upraised face and proud stance perfectly captured the book's protagonist. At least for the first half of the story.

All Vic's work, except this one book, had been detective novels, but in these eight hundred pages, she'd woven a story that spoke far more than her dozen bestsellers ever could. It might be fiction, but in it, Lane had seen Vic. And himself.

Sophie reached for the book. "Can I hold it?"

Lane hesitated. Of his meager possessions, this was one of his most treasured. It marked a turning point in his life. No one else had held this book since Vic handed it to him two and a half years ago. But she would want her daughter to know this story. If she were here, she'd have given Sophie the book herself.

There were other copies. He'd find a different one for Sophie, one a bit less fragile.

Sophie's hope-filled face and open hands waited for his answer.

The day Vic gave him this book, she'd been partway through rereading it for the tenth time. He didn't know much about writers. Vic was the first he'd met. He'd thought rereading a story, especially one she'd written, was odd—until he'd learned how much writing it had changed her. He remembered Vic's knowing smile as she sat on the park bench reading, checking on Sophie every few minutes as the little girl played on the slides and swings mere steps away. He hadn't understood why she'd given him this story back then, hadn't known what to make of a book so far outside his typical reading habits. Vic was always doing little things he didn't know what to make of. When asked, she would just smile, and light would fill her eyes. He'd only known Vic for six months before she died, but in that short span, she and Sophie had become like family to him. They'd taken him in when no one else would. Only Vic would have thought to help a nearly perfect stranger even while she battled a life-stealing disease. Sophie too had astounded him. She'd shown him kindness when others far older than her had given him no more than disapproving stares.

Sophie was barely five when her mother died. She remembered more than Lane expected her to, but there was so much about Vic that her little girl would never know. The least he could do was share this wonderful story—this piece of Vic —with her daughter.

Carefully, he laid the book in Sophie's hands.

Sophie flipped through the word-filled pages in wonder. "Mommy wrote all this?"

Lane nodded. "This story meant a lot to her. She wanted you to hear it when you got older."

Sophie hugged the book close and retreated to the couch. She looked at Lane with pleading eyes. "Will you read it to me?"

She wasn't likely to understand most of it, but children often saw things adults couldn't. Perhaps she would find the beautiful heart of this redemption story, despite all the grown-up words. She'd seen past his stoic exterior on many occasions. What made him think this cherished part of her mother was beyond her?

"Please?" Sophie maintained her death grip on the book.

"What about the park?" When he'd told her fifteen minutes ago they could go out today, she'd raced to get ready.

Sophie looked from the door to Lane. "Can we go tomorrow?"

It wasn't supposed to rain for the rest of the week. "Sure."

Sophie cradled the book as Lane settled beside her and spread her mother's favorite blanket over her lap. The blue-and-green checkered material was thick and warm.

Lane held out a hand, waiting until Sophie was ready to return the book.

The moment the rough spine and creased back cover settled into his palm, the memory of Vic giving it to him that day in the park returned fresh. The smell of damp dirt; the late March air—brisk, but not too cold; the rush of traffic just on the other side of the parking lot; Vic's quiet joy as she turned yellowed pages.

"Ready?" He said it just as much for himself as for Sophie.

The little girl leaned over the title page and nodded.

As Lane read the first few words aloud, Sophie listened intently. When he finished the first paragraph, he paused. Across the room, Vic's photo still sat in its place. Her vibrant face held a gladness he was just beginning to understand.

Sophie tapped his shoulder. "Aren't you gonna keep going?"

He swallowed past the knot in his throat. "Sorry." He smoothed the old page and kept reading.

Sophie's eyes tracked each phrase.

Vic might not be here, but in the pages of this book, she'd left a bit of herself behind.

Lane would read it as many times as Sophie asked him to.

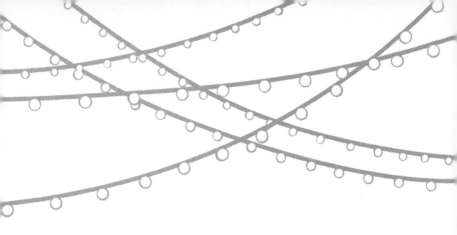

OUR GREAT REFINER

SHANA BURCHARD

"We are forsaken,
We are alone."

We heard the lonely echoes
As they encircled
Around our hearts

The threads of lonely solitude
In need
Of a welder's spark

OUR GREAT REFINER

Your far-off cry
Met my desire
And soon our flame was lit

Oh, to be welded together
We prayed in fervor
May our will be His

Our Great Refiner
Sanctifying us
Through testings and fire bold

Removing all
Our unholy dross
To reflect His image in gold

Let us show His love
Unto the world
By mirroring His compassion

Come, sweet child
Do not hesitate
By His love we've been fashioned

These ties we forge
Are made eternal
By bonds of steadfast love

Whether here on earth
And seen by others
Or among the angels above

When the shadows
Of this dreadful world
Seem to overtake our gaze

We pause
To remember our Great Refiner
And the eternity of His ways

Let us not forget
The promises etched
On His heart toward His creation

Never to leave
Nor forsake us
To love us in absolution

And so these ties we forge
Are simply echoes
Of God's love toward wanderers

They are remembrances
Of His lowly heart
A gentle and meek nature

OUR GREAT REFINER

Come, sweet child
Truth is waiting
These lies are not your destiny

Forget this mortality
And remember God's calling
Press on toward His honesty

These ties we forge
Are built to stand
The test of "Father Time"

And prove him
To be a liar
For God's love is divine

No force on earth
Could ever corrode
A love that has no end

Turn to rust
You lying shadows
May God's truth be as tungsten

Let the dross
Of loneliness
Be burned away for good

Our Father in Heaven
Is watching
And works all things for His good

And so the echoes
Answer back
From voices found in their new homes

"We will never be forsaken,
We will never be alone"

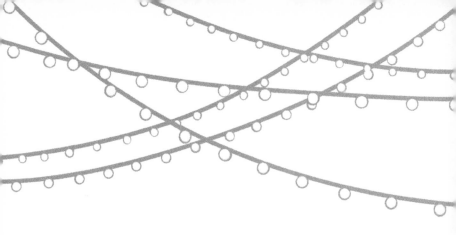

ONE DAY AT A TIME

ANNE J. HILL

Rain drizzled off the rock and thudded on Boyer's boot, over and over. Lightning cracked apart the night sky and cast shadows on their alcove in the mountainside. Thunder rumbled like a roar from a dragon-god casting judgment. The rock protected them from the worst of the rain. Boyer's horse bumped his shoulder with its nose, antsy in the storm. But Boyer, confusion and hurt stirring his stomach, was focused on the elf standing in front of him—the woman he was just beginning to have feelings for.

It was too soon to call it love, only three months. He hadn't been sure he ever could do that again. Love. Not after losing someone to the blade. But with Katollia, he had thought he might just get there again.

But then, she spoke the two words that changed Boyer's whole world.

"I'm pregnant."

Her head dipped low and she shifted uneasily. Her pointed ears grazed past her hair.

Boyer blinked. Several long beats passed before he finally said, "You're . . . you're positive? How?" It certainly hadn't been his doing.

Katollia wrapped her arms around her stomach. Her dress danced across her shoes. "It's hard to know for certain but . . . I think so. It happened before we met." Her tone was stilted as if she'd rehearsed these lines. The last time he'd seen her so withdrawn, absent from the moment, was when she'd plunge into dark memories and glaze over.

His chest tightened. "*Him*?" He held back a savage growl. The man who had hurt her . . . The one who had caused the scars covering her body.

Katollia swallowed. "Yes. I'm sorry. I didn't realize I was . . ." She rubbed her arm, tracing a scar. "I understand if you are no longer interested in me."

How could he not be interested in her? He wasn't sure that would ever change . . . but a baby? While most men his age were already fathers and providing for their families, Boyer never imagined he'd be asked to care for another man's child. He could never pretend the baby was his, either. Boyer was a human; Katollia and the father were elves. The baby would have vibrant hair, piercing eyes, sharp edges, pointed ears, and would be lean and tall. Nothing like Boyer's bulky stature, rough hands, gruff and ruddy-olive look. Everyone would know this was not his child. Even if he were to someday marry Katollia and raise the child as his own, people would know. They would assume the worst. People always did.

Boyer took a shuddering breath.

What he would have given to have been raised with a father who loved him and a mother who lived. He wouldn't have cared where they were from or the blood flowing through their veins.

Before him stood a woman he could see himself someday vowing to love and cherish through the worst in life. A child was not even close to the worst that could happen to them.

Boyer leaned in and rested his forehead against hers. "I'm still interested."

She let out a breath. "Are you sure? It won't be easy."

Nothing in Boyer's life had been easy, and he doubted it ever would be. "I know. I expect it'll be rather difficult, and I know nothing about children. But I'd still like to continue courting you, Katollia." And if things worked out for them, he'd help her raise the baby. But the notion seemed too *big* to verbalize. Not yet. One day at a time.

Boyer and Katollia are from Anne J. Hill's
upcoming debut novel, Thorn Tower.

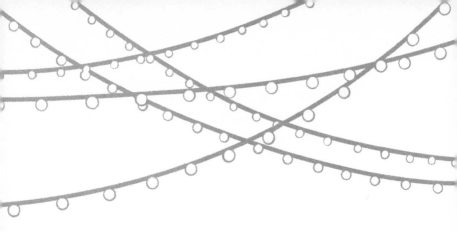

SHE AND I

MASEEHA SEEDAT

12:06 am
She wakes up
Crying and wriggling,
Searching the bed for Teddy.
I pull the stuffed animal from under my head
And wrap my arms around her instead.

05:23 am
She leaps from the blankets
Banging and slamming,
Searching the drawers for porridge.
I drag myself away from the warmth of my bed
And race to the kitchen to toast some bread.

SHE AND I

08:47 am
She races around the room
Laughing and screaming,
Squealing as I shove on a sock.
I hold her firmly, buckle the shoes
And run, for there's no time to lose.

11:11 am
She interrupts my thoughts
Babbling and jabbering,
Going on without a breath.
I pull into the checkout queue
And suddenly remember I need shampoo.

01:52 pm
She throws the pasta across the room
Wailing and complaining,
Shrieking until she's red in the face.
I quickly give her some backup mini pies
And pick the spaghetti off the tiles.

04:31 pm
She's at it again
Acting and playing,
Re-reading her favorite farm book.
I slurp the fake tea she pours
And add a point to her tic-tac-toe score.

07:23 pm
She's soaking wet
Splashing and dripping,
Leaving a soggy trail of footprints behind her.
I wrestle a diaper on
And try to convince her we're playing salon.

09:08 pm
She's still up
Eating and fussing,
Watching that purple dinosaur *again*.
I zone out of his annoying song
And she starts to sing along.

10:12 pm
She bawls her eyes
Howling and crying,
Nagging me for one more story.
I hand her Teddy, turn off the light
And the darkness eases away her fight.

11:59 pm
She finally yawns
Snuggling and cuddling,
Whispering 'I love you' in my ear.
I almost cry and bite my lip tight
And that made it all worth it tonight.

12:06 am

She's up again

I open my eyes, the first time of ten.

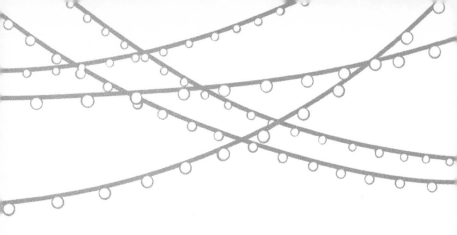

FAIREST HEIR

H. L. DAVIS

Rhosyn? Rhosyn, where are you?" I shake my head, my slippered feet treading noiselessly down the corridor. Who would have thought a simple game of hide-and-seek with a small child could last so long? I have searched nearly everywhere in the castle for my charge and even quietly enlisted the help of two other servants.

But still no sign of her.

"Rhosyn!" A sharp whisper is all I can manage as my exasperation rises, fringed with fear. Because Rhosyn *knows* we are not to wander this part of the castle, and I am now so close to rooms forbidden to me. Forbidden to *her*.

The chambers of Queen Isolde. Rhosyn's mother.

My enemy.

I had hoped when Isolde married my grieving father that I would find happiness again. But the enchantress seduced and destroyed him, seizing control of the kingdom. *My* kingdom. Then she made me a servant to my half sister. Since the day of Rhosyn's birth, I've been forced to tend to her every whim and need, to treat her as the princess and heir that I was destined to be.

And now, this miserable role of nursemaid has brought me here.

The entrance to the queen's private quarters stands just a few feet away. An icy chill grips my heart, colder than the snow for which I am named. But I clench my shaking hands into fists and force my feet to approach the rooms I once knew so well. *Surely not,* I tell myself. *Surely Rhosyn has more sense.* But as I draw closer in the dim light, all desperate reasoning dies away.

The door is ajar, a soft glow seeping through the crack into the passageway.

I take a deep breath and glance around. There is no hint of anyone. I creep to the door and slowly push it open

The changes to my mother's old bedchamber are startling. Once adorned in merry greens and golds and awash in sunlight, the room is as different now as the queen who occupies it. Burning black candles illuminate the space, standing tall in silver candelabras. The walls are draped in crimson, the large bed piled high with luxurious silks and velvet pillows to match. Across from the bed is a dressing table, its surface almost entirely covered with rows of bottled perfumes and potions. And, most unusual of all, the mirror at the back of the table is concealed beneath a dark cloth.

I lose track of the moments I stand there, feeling queasy yet mesmerized at this scene before my eyes. But my purpose returns to me when I spot the one thing out of place in the room: a bit of ice-blue fabric sticking out from beneath the bed. I close the door.

"Rhosyn? You know you're not supposed to be here. It's against the rules." I kneel and look under the bed.

There she is. Curled up in a ball, fast asleep, her blonde curls almost glowing in the shadows beneath the bed. She must've grown bored waiting for me all this while. A mixture of annoyance and relief escapes my lips in a sigh.

"Wake up." I reach out to tap her shoulder. "We must—"

Footfalls click down the corridor.

There is no mistaking the confidence and rhythm of that step.

I slip under the bed beside Rhosyn, making sure we are both fully concealed from view. Squeezing my eyes shut, I pray she doesn't wake and make noise. My chest tightens, begging for giant gulps of air.

Why, oh *why* did Rhosyn come here?

The footsteps stop. I feel the faintest draft as the door opens, another as it shuts. A rustle of skirts brushes across the rug, followed by the gentle swish of fabric near the dressing table.

"Mirror, mirror, on the wall, who is fairest of them all?"

Isolde's voice sends shivers down my spine. It's like a snake. Smooth. Charming.

Dangerous.

"A visit so soon, my queen," comes a deep reply.

"That need not concern you." Though calm, Isolde's words are laced with venom. "Only answer me, slave."

"My queen, as I have assured you for the last six years, *you* are the fairest of them all."

She sighs contentedly.

"For now."

A stillness, silent but seething, fills the room. Perspiration runs down my neck. Then, like a crack in glass, Isolde asks, "What do you mean?"

"There is another who will soon surpass you. A beauty of face to match her growing beauty of heart."

"And who, pray tell, is she?"

"The heir to the throne."

My heart jumps, and my eyes shoot to Rhosyn slumbering beside me. Completely unaware of her present danger.

"My own child. Yes." There is a note of weariness in Isolde's voice. "But I can make no exceptions."

Fingers snap, then my stepmother exits the room, the door clicking shut behind her. I wait until her footsteps fade to unleash a horrified gasp, my mind reeling with pointless questions.

Would Isolde really harm Rhosyn? *Kill* her only child?

In a heartbeat.

I close my eyes, take a shaky breath.

I cannot let that happen.

For five years, I've wrestled with my feelings toward my half sister, but things are now surprisingly, undeniably clear: Rhosyn is not to blame for the queen's mistreatment of me, for her mother's dangerous rule over my kingdom. Strangely enough, in many ways, she's been a ray of light in my life. An unexpected gift that has slipped her way into my heart.

"Eira?"

The whisper jerks me from my thoughts, and I look at Rhosyn.

"You're upset." Her voice trembles slightly, her large blue eyes glued to mine. "Are you very angry with me?"

I force a small smile. "No, Rhosyn. Not with you." I take her hand, ready to do everything in my power to protect her.

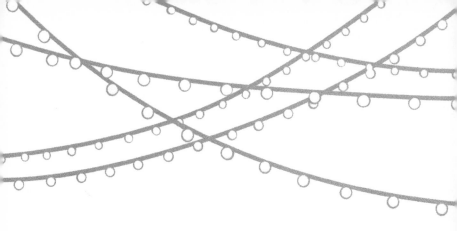

A FAR-OFF CRY

ANNE J. HILL

She crawls out of bed before the break of dawn
Stumbles through the darkness to the far-off cry
Half dazed, she trips over a lion-shaped rattle
Gathering herself, she tiptoes into the nursery

Scoops the blond baby boy from his crib
The cries fade as he snuggles to her chest
She pats his bum and whispers into his ear
Just how deeply her love for him runs

Though she did not carry him in her womb
But has tenderly carried him in her arms

Since the day he graced her with his life
She's now who she always longed to be

With a warm bottle and a soft melody
And the shushing of the sound machine
She cradles him back to sleep
In the safety of her arms

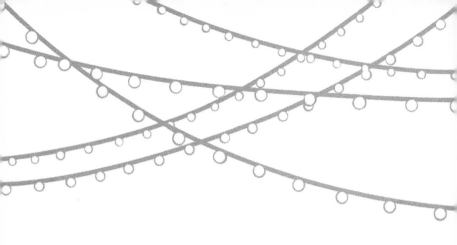

KEEPER OF ABANDONED DREAMS

ANDREA RENAE

I vo struggled to keep up with the loping strides of his new master. The ancient man cleared entire gardens with one step, the grasses and flowers bowing at his passing.

"Keep up, child. The Moment approaches," the man called, not unkindly, as he disappeared behind a building.

A panicked gasp inflated Ivo's lungs as he bounded over a rosebush and skidded around the corner. He couldn't let this opportunity get away from him, not after watching so many other children find homes—children who were far younger and more adorable than him. He needed to prove that he was the right choice.

The boy yelped as he careened into the man's side. "Sorry, Master Anselm! I didn't see—"

But Anselm held a finger to his lips and unearthed a battered book from within his woolen overcoat.

The boy gawked at the unassuming volume, then the derelict building that faced them. Fear surged at the sight of its crooked front door, held in place by a plank nailed across its frame. He gulped.

This place?

Only days ago, Ivo had been in an orphanage not so different in appearance. But this grim old man had shown up looking for an apprentice. Ivo had hung around the back of the crowd, ducking his awkward, eleven-year-old frame as best as he could, certain the outcome would be the same as all the other times. But the man's eyes were keen, and the moment they stopped on him, Ivo's heart lurched in his chest.

He chose me.

It was ridiculous, befuddling even. And Ivo knew he couldn't give Anselm a chance to rethink his decision.

The sounds of quiet sobbing reached Ivo from within the house, bringing him back to the present. As he watched the tattered rags flutter behind the broken windowpanes, he tried to stuff down his emotions.

"Are you sure you're supposed to be *here*?" he asked, risking his new master's displeasure.

But the man only nodded as he flipped through the small book.

Ivo bit back his disappointment. This was not what he expected from Anselm Walker, the most skilled Collector in all the worlds—although he hadn't even bothered asking what his apprenticeship would require before agreeing to join him. But what did he care? *Anything* was better than where he came from. And with a master as renowned as Anselm, it surely meant visiting beautiful empresses, meeting mighty warriors, and witnessing the most exciting feats in all the galaxy's histories. He'd give up anything for greatness like that.

But this place . . . this couldn't be anything important.

A hush fell on Ivo's ears, and he forgot his disappointment as he witnessed the magic of a Collecting for the first time. His master rested his hand on the open book, held it forward, and bowed his head. The world froze all around—unfortunate for the fly Ivo flicked out of its trajectory.

A soft haze of aquamarine particles trickled through the missing glass panels, swirling above the open book until it formed a solid, quivering shape, like a piece of the sky itself. Ivo thought it looked like an artist's brush, and he caught a faint whiff of oil paints before Anselm uttered a soft word and the book sucked the dream into its pages. Time ticked forward again, and the fly pancaked on a passing vehicle.

The weeping inside the building intensified for a moment, but quickly stilled. Ivo dared to peek through a gap in the curtains. A few beautiful paintings lined a grimy counter. Every other item in the room was fit for the dumpster, except for an artist's easel and a carefully arranged collection of multicolored tubes and brushes.

A young woman was packing the items reverently into a box, one by one, tears streaming down her face. But then she straightened, dried her eyes, and turned to pick up something from a laundry basket at her feet. Pressing a small bundle to her chest, the woman sighed and swayed back and forth. The bundle issued a mewling cry, and the woman shushed and hummed a lullaby that made Ivo's heart ache with emptiness.

"We'll get through this, sweet one," she whispered when her song concluded. "As soon as Mama sells these things, we'll find a better place." Her sad eyes trailed over her collection. "Art school can wait."

Ivo glanced up at Anselm, whose broad chest rose and fell with a heavy sigh as he closed the book and turned away from the scene.

When master and apprentice were several blocks away, Anselm finally spoke.

"The dreams I collect are the ones people have given up, the ones that leave a gaping hole. They are what people have chosen to sacrifice in order to focus on the needs of the moment. *Those* forgotten dreams hold more power than any achieved by ambitious deeds. And they are the ones that are most worthy of safeguarding."

They began walking again, this time at a slower pace. Shame filled Ivo as he realized how quick he had been to judge the run-down home as unworthy of Master Anselm's visit.

The circumstances may have been rough, but the woman and baby within didn't deserve to be judged by outward appearances. Anselm hadn't dismissed him, had he?

But now Ivo was pretty sure he should have.

Ivo kicked at stray pebbles, oblivious to the vibrant world around him. A question burned in his chest. He stopped and found the courage to look up at his master's face again.

"How can you tell which dreams are worth collecting? And why bother keeping them at all? Wouldn't people be better off if they could pretend they'd never existed?"

Anselm's eyes glistened, and Ivo noticed how their piercing blue matched the color of the siphoned dream.

"It's often when dreams have been fully sacrificed for another, better, higher calling that they become precious. One day—it could be a year from now, or it could be decades—the woman might find the path open to pursue that once-forgotten dream with a clear conscience because she did not abandon those she loves to attain it."

He smiled and bent forward so he could look Ivo in the eyes. "Don't we owe it to her to keep it safe until then?"

When Ivo nodded, Anselm stood and moved on. But the frown did not leave the boy's face. He stared at the ground. "And what about me? How could you tell I was worth . . . collecting?"

Anselm spun on the spot and returned to Ivo in a single step. His face was somber. "No, child. Never say such a thing again. You are not mine. I did not collect you."

"So why am I here? I'm not worth anything." *No one could ever want to remember me.*

A laugh burst from the man's lungs, startling Ivo at first, then covering him in warmth like a thick blanket. Anselm knelt before him, holding his arms out wide. "Ivo, no matter what life has taught you, you are not an afterthought, a waste of time, or a simple commodity. Your existence is the most miraculous thing in the universe. And although you may have given up the dream of being loved, someone, somewhere, must have kept it safe for you. Because today, it's come true."

Aquamarine speckles twinkled like fireworks in Anselm's gaze as Ivo threw himself into his embrace.

Tears slipped down the Collector's wrinkled cheeks. "And you, Ivo Walker, are precious."

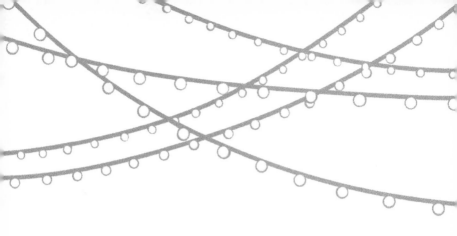

I'M STILL HERE

NATALIE NOEL TRUITT

Thunder shakes her room.
A sob chokes in her throat
as she curls around her stuffed animal,
hoping he will keep the monsters away.
She imagines her mother's arms around her,
holding her safe and keeping her warm—
what her ragged blanket fails to do on these cold winter nights.
Her mother was simply an illusion.
Her mother is now but a memory,
a ghost that follows her around.
It wakes her up in the morning,
tells her to get ready for school,

watching as she does her own hair.
She looks for breakfast, knowing the cabinets will be empty.
When was the last time I ate breakfast?

Her dad is still asleep,
or maybe not even home;
she isn't sure.
The bus comes.
Her mother kisses the top of her head
and waves as she makes sure she reaches the bus.
She does not wave back; she knows the bus full of children
would laugh if she waved to an empty house.
Daddy forgot to give her lunch money.
She sits on the playground,
waiting for the end of the day . . .
waiting until she can go home and color
while her mother watches over her
and strokes her hair.
Her dad's on the phone when she walks through the door;
he doesn't come to say hi.
Does he remember that I'm still here?
Her torn clothes and the empty dinner table
provide the answer.
Night comes around.
He showers and tries to braid her hair,
while she pretends it is her mother's fingers weaving
her locks together.

I'M STILL HERE

Lights flash from the gravel driveway.
Unfamiliar arms wrap around her,
carrying her from her bedroom
and out of the front door
into her new life.

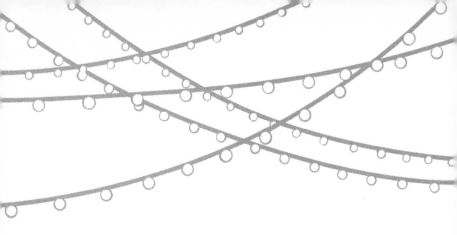

THE RUNAWAY

MORGAN J. MANNS

I had always dreamt of running away but never had the guts to actually do it. Instead, after years spent hating my existence, I yearned for my eighteenth birthday. I thought if I could at least make it to that coveted adulthood milestone, my past could be put behind me. That hope shattered when my father's rage landed me in the hospital with fractured ribs and a broken nose—all because I forgot to pick up milk on my way home from school. There was no way I was going back to that house. Once I regained enough strength, I seized my chance and fled.

Running out of that hospital was the moment I'd yearned

for. Finally stepping into the reality of my daydreams, I was free.

Turning away from my unkempt appearance in the reflection of the bus window and rubbing the scruff around my chin, I reach into my jean pocket and count through the loose change, holding each coin like the lifeline it is. After two careful recounts, I close my hands and press my fist against my forehead. It is barely enough to get me to the next bus station. Stupid of me to believe I could survive on my own. Truly stupid.

Leaning back against the leather headrest, I remind myself I'm still better off than I was two weeks ago. As bleak and uncertain as my current situation is, *home* is ten times worse. My family never cared about me. The bruises were proof enough.

A man a few seats behind me snores roughly, then coughs in his sleep. I release a tight-chested sigh. Another bus. Another night among a sea of strangers. I keep my black hoodie up over my mess of cropped curls and slide deeper into my seat. Hopefully, I'm not recognized from the missing-child notices I'm sure my parents begrudgingly sent across the country.

I look out the window, glimpsing barren, moonlit fields. I'll find a way to remain hidden and keep moving forward. I don't exactly know how, but something inside me insists I must. Maybe I can get a job as a farmhand somewhere around here—I've seen plenty of farms dotting the landscape on the long bus rides across the countryside. Surely, the farmers wouldn't care that I don't have a resume to hand them.

My fingers trace absentminded lines along the frost rimming the bus window. As hard as each day is, returning to my family is the only option I won't consider. I'm merely a mistake in their eyes—a recurring burden, as they keep reminding me. I hug myself tightly. At least in a few months, I'll finally turn eighteen and be free of them. Until that day arrives, survival is the only thing that matters.

I run a hand wearily down my face. I should probably rest. Scrounging for food and warmth will be challenging enough without the cloud of exhaustion currently hovering over me.

The heaviness of my eyelids and the motion of the bus lulls me into a restless sleep. Haunting memories rake over my dreams, molding them into nightmares. Angry parents. Unrelenting fear. Abuse. My ribs are broken anew.

Enough! I awake in a cold sweat, turning my head wildly, reminding myself of where I am. *They're not here. They're not here* . . . I rub my chest, repeating my mantra, giving up on sleep. As broken as I was, they can't hurt me now. Not here.

Resigned to exhaustion, I set my gaze on the monochromatic scenery flashing by—late autumn's bare trees, harvested fields, frost-covered cattails along ditches—all preludes to winter.

Despite the heat blowing through the vents at my feet, I shiver. I still can't believe I accidentally left my jacket on the last bus. My teeth clench as I form my hands into fists. With the small amount of money I have left, there's no way I can afford another one. Stupid of me. Stupid.

Shifting in my seat, I force myself to make a plan. Maybe I could steal one. I look at the sleeping people around me. Perhaps even from someone on this bus. The thought has my heart racing with nervous anticipation.

I decide I'm going to do it. I'm going to do something I've never done before. Steal.

But, before I can act, another terrible cough rattles from the man behind me. He curses under his breath. Apparently, I'm not the only one who can't sleep. There's no way I can snatch something if he's watching.

I chance a quick glance over my shoulder to see if he's actually awake. The bearded man is in the midst of clearing his throat, knocking a fist against his chest as if to help clear it. Our eyes meet, and a deep furrow forms on his wrinkled brow.

I cringe, knowing what that look means—I've seen it from my father a thousand times. He's about to teach me a lesson. Swallowing the lump in my throat, I turn back around, sliding deeper into my seat. *Stupid! Don't draw attention to yourself! Especially from guys who look like they belong in biker gangs.*

Too late. I smell him before I see him. The foul scent—a mix of cigarette smoke and alcohol—hits me like a putrid perfume. Unintentionally, I flinch, pulling my hoodie up to cover my face just to get away from the stench. *Wrong move, idiot.*

"What are you staring at, boy?" he growls, leaning over. His hands are on the seats, trapping me.

Panicked, I manage, "Nothing, sir."

He sways dangerously close. "You've got a problem, boy? I see the way you're hiding." He juts his bulbous face toward me.

Frozen, I notice some of the passengers have roused from their sleep. I glance toward the few in my line of sight, wordlessly asking for help. My fearful gaze is met with apologetic indifference. They look away, pretending not to see. Heat rises to my cheeks, turning my fear into anger. I shouldn't be surprised—the world has always turned its back on me.

The man removes his hand from the seat in a swift move and clenches the scruff of my hoodie. My gaze snaps back to him and I suck in a breath.

He pulls me close. "I asked you what your problem is!"

Without warning, brakes screech, and the bus swings sideways.

The man holding me stumbles back into the aisle, taking me with him. He widens his stance and manages to keep hold of my hoodie. I go along with his movements like a helpless puppet. A few nervous heartbeats later, the bus rolls to a stop on the side of the road.

The abrupt change in motion has the rest of the passengers waking up, looking around with groggy groans and raised eyebrows. Soon, everyone's eyes are on us.

The man turns his gaze toward the front of the bus, breathing like a raging bull. He still has me in a death grip and I'm afraid to move, not wanting to draw any further attention to myself.

A voice echoes down the long aisle from near the front of the bus. "Enough, Jerry. Let the boy go." It sounds like the driver. I remember his friendly "hello" from when I boarded the bus. His voice holds no friendly cheer now.

Wait. Did he stop the bus for *me*?

A tense moment goes by. Then, Jerry's grip loosens and I slump back onto the seat. I rub my neck, still feeling the ghost of the man's hand near my throat.

"He started it, Gord." Jerry points an accusing finger in my direction, sounding like a dumb middle-school bully. "You should have seen the way he was staring—judging me like he's better." He shakes his finger in emphasis. "Look at him. He's the worthless one. Homeless by the looks of it. Go back to driving, I'll deal with this scum."

I close my eyes, wondering if this is another nightmare I haven't woken from yet.

"You've no right starting fights on my bus. And if you pick one with a minor, you're definitely going back to jail."

I reopen my eyes, seeing fear in Jerry's.

Gord continues, his voice level but firm. "Get off my bus,

cool down, and I'll swing back to pick you up after dropping this lot off in town."

Jerry's shoulders heave in time with his growling breath. The way he's tensed, I think he's going to pummel the smaller man.

"Go, Jerry. Before you do something you'll regret." The driver steps to the side, gesturing to the front. A clear dismissal.

With a grumble, Jerry reaches into his seat to grab his jacket before storming past us and off the bus.

Gord turns and presses his lips together in a thin line. "Hey, sorry about all that. Jerry's a regular on this route, and, well . . . That man makes some poor choices." His eyebrows crease together with concern and his voice softens. "Are you . . . okay?"

I still feel Jerry's hand at my throat. Am I okay? I'm not sure. "I'll . . . I'll be alright," I say, but even I'm not convinced by my words.

Gord peers at me and rubs his chin as if he's trying to make a decision. After a moment, he says, "Listen, kid, I don't know where you're headed, but take this." He shrugs off his jacket and hands it to me. "I noticed you didn't have one when you boarded. Winter's around the corner, you know." He grins.

My eyes widen at the unexpected gesture. Before he changes his mind, I shakily accept the heavy woolen coat and nod, offering him a small smile in return.

He tips an invisible hat toward me and returns to the driver's seat.

I release a breath and put on the jacket, feeling its immediate warmth. It takes a moment to realize I'm safe, that no one is about to pound me into oblivion. That's a first.

As the bus turns back onto the highway, I glance outside. Jerry's on the side of the road, glaring directly at me. The bus moves past him and he kicks the gravel in our wake.

Soon, he disappears from view and I sigh with relief. Looking to the front, Gord is focused on the highway, occasionally glancing at me through the rearview mirror. The tightness in my chest loosens and my lips pull into a small, disbelieving grin. Someone is watching over me.

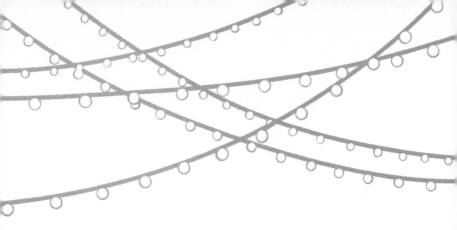

ORPHANED BUT NOT FATHERLESS

ALI NOËL

We have been charged, commanded
We know what pure religion is
Look after the orphans in their distress
Wars have been waged
so long, too long
Hear my fervent plea!
Bend a willing ear
War is more than
bloodied fields, razed concrete
War is souls torn asunder, greedy hands
Blind-eyes turned as
children are sold for the night

Far be it from us
to lose the precious in the crossfires
Take your stand, I'll take mine
Holding hands with the souls
who have no safe knees to sit upon
No closet-checker, bully-fighter
I want to be a mouthpiece
not a blindfold
He will not leave you
He will come to you
Church—no matter your conviction
Do not leave them
Come to them
One need not look far

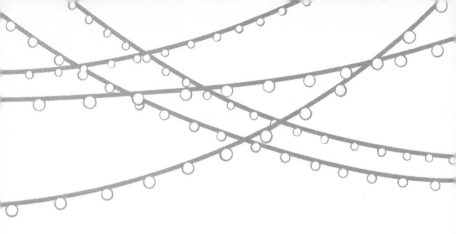

WHERE THE
FLAMES DIE

ANNIE LOUISE TWITCHELL

Theo winced, dropped the wrench, and glared at his thumb, then the lug nuts on the tire. He'd set out to fight with the truck, and the truck had chosen to fight back. Just a scrape, but still annoying.

"Anderson!" Cap's voice rang out across the engine bay. "Report to the office. ASAP!"

Theo muttered under his breath, scooped up the wrench, and tried to tighten the lug nut he'd just attempted to loosen. The wrench didn't budge one way or the other and he made a mental note to find the can of lubricant in the maintenance room. That task would have to wait until after this meeting with Cap. What had he done now?

Placing the wrench back into the tool kit, he closed the case and stowed it back in the cabinet on the engine. *Always leave things ready to run.* That was one of the first rules he'd learned at Station 5, although it was second nature to him from a lifetime of running.

Theo grabbed a thick blue paper towel from the roll on the wall by the eye-wash station and scrubbed at the grease on his hands as he headed toward the living quarters and offices.

"Anderson!" Cap bellowed again, sounding uncharacteristically impatient.

"Coming, sir," Theo wadded up the paper towel and threw it in the trash barrel near the stairs. He took them two at a time, almost running into Cap at the top of the steps.

"Chief wants to see you." Cap jerked a thumb over his shoulder at the chief's office. "You look like a grease monkey, man. What in the world were you doing?"

"Trying to change out the tire on the squad truck, sir. It's got a slow leak. Lt. told me to change it out for the spare and get the main into the garage to be checked and patched."

Cap grunted, eyeing Theo's dark blue tactical pants and black tee shirt covered in dust and grime. "I'll handle it. Get going."

Theo nodded and strode across the training room toward Chief's office, his stomach flip-flopping. For all the times his captain had called him a problematic, loud-mouthed kid, Theo had only ever been called into the chief's office once before. That was two years ago when he was bumped up from probie to firefighter-paramedic at the ripe old age of twenty-three.

He knocked on the black wooden door with CHIEF emblazoned across the surface in white paint.

"Come in."

Chief Ryan O'Neill was younger than most fire chiefs in the area. At forty-five years old, he was still an active-duty firefighter. If the situation called for extra manpower, he had been known to turn command over to his deputy chief, Rick Butler, and go into the fire. Butler, about twelve years O'Neill's senior, had been a firefighter since before Theo was born and possibly since before Theo's mom was born. Rick and Chief made a good team. They were always on the ground cleaning trucks and washing hoses after a call, too, instead of going to the office. They worked as hard as the rest of the crew and handled the paperwork and reports on top of it, and there were few men Theo respected more.

Chief was sitting behind his desk. Three chairs faced him. On either end sat Rick and a uniformed police officer from Westbrook, a town about an hour away. The chair in between was empty, and Chief beckoned Theo to it. "Have a seat."

Theo hesitated. "Can I ask what this is about, sir?" He tried to hide the uncertainty in his voice, but it was a vain effort.

Chief raised an eyebrow and gestured again to the chair. Theo understood the silent command, although he did not like it. He sat but refused to relax, drumming his fingers on his knee.

"Theo," Chief began.

Theo's heartbeat immediately quickened as adrenaline punched through his gut. No one at the station called him by his first name. His last name—the name he had chosen when he was sixteen years old, when his mom and dad finalized the adoption—was the name he preferred to use at the station.

"We have some bad news," Chief continued. "I'm not going to beat around the bush. You deserve better."

"What happened?" The words came out in a hoarse croak.

Deputy Chief Butler leaned over and rested a strong hand on Theo's shoulder as if to brace him for impact.

"Your sister Sonya was killed in a car accident in Westbrook this morning."

Theo stared at Chief, then shook his head. "She's in San Francisco."

"No, Theo. She flew in last night and was driving up here to visit. A semi truck ran the red light and hit her rental car."

Theo stood, pushing Butler's hand away. "That—that's not possible. That's not possible."

"I'm sorry, Mr. Anderson," the uniform said from the other chair.

"She's in San Francisco!" Theo slammed his fist on Chief's desk. "She's staying in California until the baby is born."

The realization hit him a second after the pain in his fist.

He dropped back into the chair. "The baby?"

"The ER in Portland delivered the baby. She is alive and apparently doing well, although they want to keep her for several days to monitor for . . . complications." The officer cleared his throat. "The hospital says you are her power of attorney and next of kin based on her records, so you would be the child's temporary guardian since there is no information available on her father."

Complications. Theo knew what complications looked like for an infant in a car accident: bumps and bruises, hemorrhage, brain injury, damage to the soft bones that hadn't finished growing, and hundreds more. He also knew what complications looked like for a child without a parent. He had lived through those before he finally came home, but the scars never disappeared. His younger siblings, Vivi, Sonya, Abbi, and Nate, carried their own secret scars. They all knew what it was like to be alone in a boundless ocean of people.

"Theo?" Chief prompted, his voice unexpectedly gentle. "Hey. Theo."

"I gotta go," he mumbled. "Gotta go see the kid."

The officer nodded. "I can drive you. I have to go back to Westbrook and the ER is only a few minutes out of the way."

Theo stood and headed for the door. The officer exchanged a few words with Chief before following him, but Theo didn't hear. He remembered the day he had first gone to the ocean with his mom and dad, when he'd placed a huge conch against his ear and listened to the waves breaking inside the shell. His dad had spoken to him, but the words turned into the waves, too, and it was impossible to tell what was his dad's voice and what was the ocean's voice.

He felt that way now. It was impossible to tell what was the officer's voice and what was the thudding rhythm of his heart, beating its way out of his chest.

It was two days before he could hold the baby. Two days of pacing the hallways and driving the NICU nurses up a wall, two days of questions with no answers, two days of cold grief catching him by surprise.

"What do you need?" Chief asked via text. "Do you need stuff for the baby?"

Theo didn't know how to answer. Would she even leave the hospital? And should she go home with him? Would that be the best thing for her?

But at the same time, something in him knew if she left the hospital, she would be in his arms, going home with him.

If there was one thing Theo knew for certain, it was that he wanted to spend his life doing something good, something helpful. Something that would make up for at least a little of the misery in the world.

He texted Chief back to say that he would need baby stuff but didn't have any idea what specifically to get. Chief said they would take care of it, and Theo knew they would—that was what they did.

Cap sent him an email outlining the plan for the next two weeks. He had allocated all of Theo's bereavement days and sick days to his scheduled shifts so he could take off the two weeks, and they were working with the city's human resources director to get Theo the mandated six weeks of paternity leave. Besides all that, Cap said, his shift had pooled some paid vacation days for an extra four weeks off. That would give him twelve weeks from the day he had walked out of the station. Three months to figure himself out.

"Family takes care of each other," Cap said at the end of the email. "Call us if you need anything."

Finally, after the longest forty-eight hours of his life, a nurse found him sprawled across two chairs in the waiting area. "Mr. Anderson?"

Theo stopped breathing for a few seconds, staring silently up at the young man's face. The nurse smiled. "Are you ready to meet your niece?"

Theo wasn't sure he would ever set the baby down again. She fit in his arms like the missing piece of a puzzle. She'd been through so much in her very short life, but he couldn't tell from looking at her perfect little face.

She wouldn't take a bottle at first, but he and the nurses worked on it anyway. Two more days of this, of trying to feed her and listening to her hungry wails: sheer misery. Theo was constantly on edge, begging her to take the bottle. He hadn't lost this much sleep since college.

Her fourth day there—when the only major concern left was her eating—she finally accepted the bottle from him and started to drink, her big blue eyes fixed on his face.

Theo didn't realize he was crying until the tears trickled down onto her blanket.

"I love you," he whispered. "I love you so much."

The next day, they were discharged. His crew had pulled together everything they could think of for a new baby, from a crib to shopping bags of baby clothes to two boxes of diapers. Vivi and her husband Kim had helped get the baby items from the station to Theo's apartment across town. She, eight months pregnant herself, had arranged the living room and Theo's bedroom to make space.

His mom and dad came down to bring them home. They hadn't been allowed into the hospital due to the high rate of illness going around, so it had been just him for the last week. He knew that while his parents were still trying to cope with Sonya's death, they were eager to see their new grandchild.

Theo cradled the baby in his arms, taking advantage of the last few minutes alone in the hospital before his parents arrived. The little girl—perfect from her soft halo of dark hair to her ten tiny toes—blinked pale blue eyes up at him, gurgled, and blinked again. A lullaby played from his phone, low and sweet.

He hadn't chosen a name yet. The nurses said it could wait up to ten days, but it would be easier if he named her before they left the hospital.

Theo didn't have a list of baby names like Vivi did. Kim had texted him Vivi's list, with a line through the name they'd chosen for their own baby—Lucy Ann—and Theo had gone over it a dozen times in the last few days. Nothing really stood out to him.

He had thought, of course, about naming her after her mother. But he couldn't reconcile the perfect little bundle of sunshine in his arms with the temperamental teenage girl he had first met eight years ago when she was sent to live with their family, or the brave, strong woman she had grown into. Sonya had always been closest to him; out of all the mismatched siblings, they were the two who were angriest at the cards life dealt them, the two who had the 'fight' instead of 'flight' response. Giving her name to the baby would be a way to honor her, but honor and memory are not always the same thing, and he was afraid of replacing his sister with his niece.

He was afraid of a good deal more than that.

But the baby in his arms stirred, smiling into the sunlight breaking through the clouds into the hospital room. And the lullaby ended, and the next song began.

"Amazing Grace, how sweet the sound," trickled out the words of Sonya's favorite hymn.

All at once, he knew.

"Welcome home, Grace."

ACKNOWLEDGMENTS

Thank you to all the authors and poets who graciously shared their pieces with us. We could not have a book without their contributions. A big thank you to the editors (Natalie Noel Truitt, Samantha Mandell, and Claire Tucker) and the typesetter (Andrea Renae) who volunteered their services for free so that we can give more funds to the ministry. Thank you to the beta readers who pitched in to help this book shine and everyone else who poured their time and energy into this book. Thank you, Natalie, for running this anthology with me! And thank you to God for guiding us on this publishing journey.

—Anne J. Hill

Thank you to everyone who has volunteered their time and services to make this anthology what it is. We have had so many wonderful, creative people donate their talents, and I appreciate every one of them! Thank you, Anne, for doing this anthology with me and making it such a great experience. Thank you to my fiancé, Alex, for the support he gave me throughout the writing and editing process. And thank you, God, for this gift of writing.

—*Natalie Noel Truitt*

ABOUT THE AUTHORS

ANNE J. HILL

Anne J. Hill is an author who enjoys writing fantasy for all ages. Her love of words has led to her career as an editor and content writer. She runs Twenty Hills Publishing with the help of her circus performing best friend, Lara E. Madden. She spends her days dreaming up fantastical realms, researching ways to get away with murder . . . for her books, arguing over commas at the kitchen table, talking out loud to the characters in her head, promising her housemate that she isn't, in fact, crazy, and rearranging her personal library—affectionately dubbed the "Book Dungeon."

NATALIE NOEL TRUITT

 Natalie Noel Truitt is an aspiring Christian author who spends her days working at the library and adding more books to her to-be- read list. She is often on her front porch drinking coffee, reading a good book, and hanging out with her cat.

MORGAN J. MANNS

 Morgan J. Manns is a speculative fiction author who enjoys crafting enchanting worlds and captivating magic systems, a skill she nurtures after tucking her children into bed. Her imagination is fueled by the works of Brandon Sanderson, Patrick Rothfuss, & Christopher Paolini, serving as constant inspiration. By day, Morgan works as an elementary school teacher, seeking ways to ignite the writing potential in her students while helping them uncover the transformative power of the written word. When she's not writing, or teaching about writing, she can be found chasing after her two young children, delving into fantasy novels alongside her husband, or exploring the breathtaking Canadian vistas surrounding her home. One of her favorite pastimes is canoeing with her family on the small lake just behind her house. Find more of her stories at Havok Publishing or on her Instagram account, @morgan.j.manns

NATHANIEL LUSCOMBE

Nathaniel Luscombe is the author of *Moon Soul*. He's a science fantasy author from Ontario, Canada. He writes across genres, dabbles in poetry, runs anthologies, and reads an unreasonable amount of books every year. Find him on Instagram: @hecticreadinglife

YVONNE MCARTHUR

Yvonne McArthur is a writer, editor, and adventurer based in Guatemala. She's spent over a decade honing her writing skills through creative writing, blogging, and ghostwriting. Her time as a personal caregiver, foster mom, and International Justice Mission intern fueled her interest in at-risk children. Yvonne is passionate about writing stories that encourage us to be kinder, more courageous, and more connected humans. You can find her at her author blog, www.yvonnemcarthur.com, and at www.guateadventure.com, a niche travel blog helping thousands of people discover Guatemala.

HANNAH CARTER

Hannah Carter is just a girl who wakes up every day hoping to figure out she's secretly a mermaid. She is the author of *The Atlantis Trilogy*, which includes *The Depths of Atlantis* and *A Twist of Tides*. Hannah's short stories and award-winning flash fiction pieces have been published in various anthologies, and in 2022, she won a Realm Award. In addition to fiction, she also has had over a dozen devotions published. In her spare time, she's either cuddling her cats, reading with a cup of tea, or listening to an absurd amount of Taylor Swift. Connect with her on Instagram at @mermaidhannahwrites

H. L. DAVIS

H. L. Davis is a Christian, wife, and homeschool mom who calls the South home. She first discovered the joys of writing at ten years of age, and it is a craft she is delighted to pursue once again. When she isn't brainstorming ideas and weaving words into stories, she enjoys reading, graphic design, and quality time with her family and friends. You can find more of her speculative fiction at Havok Publishing or on her Instagram account, @h.l.davis_stories

SARAH ANNE ELLIOTT

Sarah Anne Elliott is a writer and artist that lives near Portland Oregon with her beautiful dog Pharaoh. She sells her art professionally online, focusing on abstract portraits and Impressionism.

Etsy: https://www.etsy.com/shop/SElliottExclusive

ANDREA RENAE

Andrea Renae is a lover of all things beautiful and rich in meaning. She believes in the power of a good story to bring hope and truth in the most unexpected ways. Her debut novel, *Where Darkness Dwells*, explores themes of depression, purpose, courage, and redemption in a fantastic world that feels strangely familiar. She hopes her words will point hungry hearts to deeper, soul-satisfying truths. You can find out more about her and her writing on her website: www.authorarenae.com

D. T. POWELL

D. T. Powell has loved stories since before she can remember, and it was love for one of those many stories that prompted her to start writing. She's worked in the fanfiction community since 2013 and continues to contribute to it regularly. While she pursues publication for her novel-length and short-form original fiction, she spends time reading, playing pickleball, and the occasional video game. Her work has been published by Writer's Digest, Clean Fiction Magazine, and Cadence Writing.

DENICA MCCALL

Denica McCall is a fantasy writer, poet, dreamer, and old soul who grew up in the Pacific Northwest and now resides in Kansas City. When not writing, she works as a nanny and a freelance editor. She also enjoys attending dance classes, visiting coffee shops, and planning her next travel adventure. She is currently working on a fantasy trilogy exploring generational themes and racial reconciliation. The trilogy features a people with the ability to turn into dust, a pegasus, and cave-stars. Find out more and sign up for her newsletter to receive a free short story at http://denicamccall.com/. Instagram Handle: @denicamcauthor

ANNIE LOUISE TWITCHELL

Annie Louise Twitchell is a writer, reader, poet, artist, journalist, first responder, and outdoor enthusiast living and working in the Western Mountains of Maine. She has received multiple awards for her writing and photography and has published more than a dozen books.

JADE LA GRANGE

Jade La Grange is a budding writer who has yet to fully discover how exactly she'll bloom in the world of writing. But while she's waiting, she's on a side quest to live a life that involves vigorously devouring all the books, overly-snuggling her precious poodles, spending quality time with her loved ones in the sunshine country of South Africa where she grew up and still currently resides, and sharpening the minds of young individuals via her additional job as a teacher with the hope that they, too, won't be afraid to pick up a pen and write to their heart's content. In other words, Jade is still very much a work in progress. And you know what? She's completely content with that. Here's to overcoming life's dragons, one wielded word at a time. Instagram: @madetobejade

BROOKE J. KATZ

Brooke J. Katz is a stay at home/homeschooling mom by day and author/poet by night. Jesus and Lyons tea fuel her. Writing and painting have been a way for her to step into another world and for her work to be an outlet for someone else to find encouragement, or just some time to themselves being lost in a story. She is known to always have a book on her and dropping what she's doing to pray. You can find her on IG/Goodreads @brookejkatz or her website https://brookejkatz.wixsite.com/brookejkatz

AUDRAKATE GONZALEZ

 AudraKate Gonzalez started writing horror stories when she ran out of Goosebumps books to read as a child. Her love for horror grew and now she has a BA in Creative Writing and is working on her MFA. Her written works include her YA Horror series, *This is Noir*, her Middle-Grade Mystery series, *Welcome to Noir*, and numerous poems and stories in various anthologies. She likes to use frequent themes of paranormal, monsters, villains, good versus evil, family values, and coming-of-age. AudraKate's books will appeal to fans of *Goosebumps*, *Fear Street*, Christopher Pike, and *Point Horror*. AudraKate is a current member of the Horror Writers Association, Sigma Tau Delta, and enjoys her time working as Editor-in-Chief at Twenty Hills Publishing. She lives in Ohio with her handsome husband, and her adorable furry bad boys, Zero and Scrappy Doo. When AudraKate isn't writing, you can find her reading, watching scary movies or sleeping. You can follow her on Instagram and TikTok @lets.get.lit.erature or check out her website www.authoraudrakategonzalez.com

C. F. BARROWS

C. F. Barrows writes to grapple with tough issues and share the good news of Jesus Christ with her generation and the next. She lives in Northern Indiana with her family and two clingy cats.

SHANA BURCHARD

 Shana Burchard lives in Northwestern Pennsylvania with her husband and two beloved children. When she's not writing articles and books, she enjoys taking walks outside, coffee dates, and laughing with friends. As a young girl, she always wanted to be a writer and would write stories in her free time. She attended Allegheny College as an English and psychology double major. She then went on to earn her master's degree in education (pedagogy and practice) from Mercyhurst University. Her first book, *The Puppy Who Could Not Bark*, was released in 2022.

MASEEHA SEEDAT

Born and raised in South Africa, Maseeha Seedat takes inspiration for her stories from the most memorable moments of her life. She's a full-time student and a part-time writer, with her first novel, *The Littlest Voices*, published a year after her publishing debut with Twenty Hills. Her writing ranges from the fun and whimsical to the dark and serious, most of the time settling somewhere in the middle. When she's not writing, Maseeha can be found surrounded by her family and friends or clawing her way toward a degree in physiotherapy.

ALI NOËL

Ali Noël lives in the greater Seattle area with her three young kinds and rambunctious bulldog. If she's not writing or having a dance party, you can find her reading, baking, or watching any take on a Jane Austen novel. Her work has been featured in Z Publishing House, SobreMesa Zine and Wow! Women on Fiction. You can find Ali and her poetry on Instagram @the.authoress.life

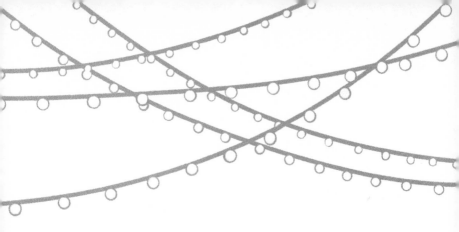

OTHER BOOKS BY TWENTY HILLS PUBLISHING

BLACK AND GOLD ANTHOLOGIES

What Darkness Fears

Fool's Honor

Sharper Than Thorns

Wither and Bloom

THE NEVER TALES

The Never Tales: Volume One

The Never Tales: Volume Two

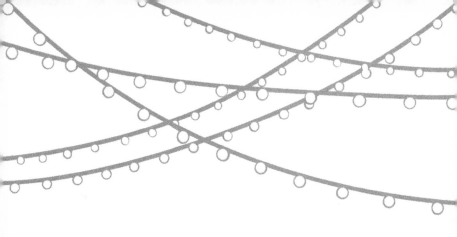

www.annejhill.com/twenty-hills-publishing

Instagram @twenty_hills

Milton Keynes UK
Ingram Content Group UK Ltd.
UKHW050914170424
441314UK00004B/94